THE EXILED

JJ ANDERS

GRAYTON
PRESS

THE EXILED

DIGITAL ISBN: 978-1-945100-44-4

PHYSICAL ISBN: 9798764731131

Published by Grayton Press

SUMMARY

Zander, the crown prince of Genoa, has grown up in a kingdom filled with magic and love. His parents, Queen Tresstéanna and King Kriston, raised him and his sisters surrounded by dragons in the east and trolls in the north, along with many more of Genoa's creatures.

When Zander, along with a handful of his fellow dragon warriors, are banished to Earth, he finds himself faced with the first real problems of his life. Zander's struggles with the technology and fast pace of Denver might be hard but discovering the magic that could return him and his fellow Genoans home might just kill them all.

Dragon warrior Reyleen, recently assigned to protect her land's prince, has known many battles. It seems, however, that guarding the self-destructive prince will be her biggest challenge. When her band of warriors, along with the prince, are thrown into the strange land Zander calls Earth, she and the queen's sorcerer, Belent, must try and keep everyone in the group safe as they attempt to find the doorway home.

To my son, who has the imagination the size of a dragon.

AUDIOBOOKS

Enjoy listening along. Grab a copy of The Scholar, The Warrior, and The Queen on Audiobook. Narrated by Marnye Young.

Links:
  Amazon
  Audible

MAP OF GENOA
JJ ANDERS

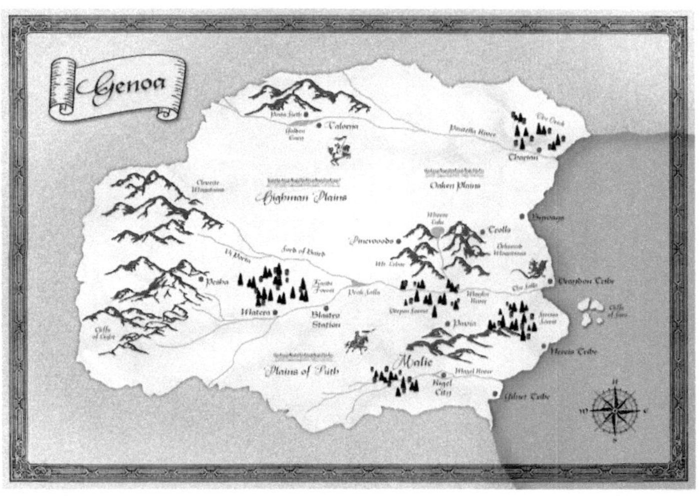

PREFACE

Tresstéanna, queen of Genoa, sat amongst her colorful and fragrant flowers and sighed. Her laithers were growing nicely now. Their pale pink faces blew gently in the air, and the purfla flowers that surrounded them made the garden smell like heaven.

Her long blond hair, now mixed with a few fine strands of gray, rustled in the cool breeze of Genoa's spring as she settled the folds of her long peach skirt against the stone bench she sat on.

She glanced up at the bright moon Blinske high above her head. It was now only a sliver, but its yellow glow was still bright in the sky. Turning to her left, she could just make out Ra Neth. The blue orb hovered above the castle walls in the growing morning sky.

Her pale blue eyes closed briefly, and she took in a deep breath of fragrant air as the warm sun shone down on her. She felt the crown on her head shift slightly and reached up to trace the white gold until her fingers touched the moon stone that sat dead center of her forehead.

She had a busy day ahead of her. The counsel was

meeting in a few short hours and then she had other conferences afterward. The royal guard needed her for their monthly inspections, and the meals for the upcoming dignitary dinner needed to be reviewed and approved. She also had to choose the wine selection to be served. Today it was hard to wake fully, and she thought that the garden and its fresh air would help.

Seth, her dear friend, and fellow dragon warrior, had requested a private meeting with her and Kriston before her day began, and she knew that she should be getting ready. But for this minute, she would continue sitting in her private garden, watching the busy bees dip in and out of her flowers while she let her mind wander.

Years had passed since her excursion down into the Kylix, the massive underground tunnel that led to the cradle, where the celestial orb of their world's deity now resided. She and a band of fellow warriors had returned Genoa safely back to the goddess's resting place and had discovered a new world, Midzark, while they were on that quest.

Midzark, inhabited by giants called the Nephilim and a smaller people called the Húriya, were now their allies. Tresstéanna and her friends had successfully aided Grand Carrington in succeeding the throne high up in the Régorge palace. The giantess had immediately decreed that all Húriya were free, and a peace had settled across that land for the first time in generations.

Tresstéanna, upon return to the mainland, had sent ambassadors to Midzark each year and, in return, Grand Carrington and her daughter Charlotte had come for a visit twice in the last ten years.

A smile crossed Tresstéanna's face when she thought of the giant girl, Charlotte. Charlotte had grown to be quite an advocate for all creatures of their world, including the massive bees that could only be found in Midzark. Carrington had told Tresstéanna, quite proudly, that her daughter had a fine garden and kept her own small hive of the bees near the palace.

Her smile faltered when Tresstéanna thought of her own daughters. She didn't worry too much about her youngest girl, Charlotte, who had been named after the Grand's daughter, but more for her oldest child, Caylee.

Caylee was a beauty with her father's dark hair and green eyes. But the girl was in a most difficult time of her life. At twenty-one, Caylee was unsure of the pathway for her personal life. She often second-guessed her abilities and her own magic. Oh, not in her royal duties, Tresstéanna thought with a shake of her head. There Caylee excelled. No, it was beyond the crown's obligations where her eldest was befuddled.

Tresstéanna had no doubt these recent problems arose mostly from the girl's new beau, Grant Worthington. Grant was a fair-haired boy who held himself with arrogance, at least in Tresstéanna's mind.

It is true, he was a handsome lad, with pale skin and a handsome face. But that face was too often set in a frown for her liking. His eyes weren't always kind and, when gazing at her daughter, seemed to hold many secrets.

Grant wouldn't be her first choice for her daughter, and unfortunately, neither she nor Kriston trusted the boy. Caylee's strong mind had been voiced during those family arguments, which is why Tresstéanna was now sequestered to her garden. Just last night, another bout of arguments had broken out and remembering the harsh words spoken caused a small headache to form. Reaching up, she rubbed her temple where the ache was spreading.

"Your face will stick like that if you continue frowning," came a rich deep voice from beside her. "And then I'll have to look at that frown on your face for the rest of my life."

A smile quickly replaced the frown as Tresstéanna turned her head to see her husband Kriston standing behind her. A cocky grin spread across his handsome face, and his green eyes twinkled with mischief as he sat next to her.

His once-black hair was now sprinkled with silver around his temples and a few stubborn grays could be found in his neatly trimmed goatee as well. There were a few wrinkles around his eyes, but to her, he looked just like the day she had met him all those years ago.

"Pray tell, what puts a frown upon Your Majesty's pretty face today," he said with a slight bow of his head.

"Don't tease." She grasped his hand. "I was thinking of Caylee."

"Ah, but despite her outcry from last night, our daughter is, at this moment, on her way to the throne room to complete her royal duties. It appears some of our words sank in last night." Kriston brought her hand to his lips for a kiss, or more like a nibble.

"Really?" Tresstéanna asked. She turned to look at the double glass doors behind her.

"No, let her be. We have our own meetings soon. But for now, let us enjoy the flowers." He gave her hand a tug, and she turned once again to face the garden. "And each other."

"Where is Zander?" she asked as she rested her head on his shoulder.

"I saw him head off with Belent towards the training yard," Kriston replied, and she felt the laugh emanate from his chest before she heard it. "Belent wants to test his magics."

"He wouldn't have to test them if our son would buckle down on using them more often," Tresstéanna stated, and another frown covered her face. But then she thought of her latest scheme with regard to her son. Tresstéanna loved Reyleen. She had known the girl since her birth and still loved the girl's parents, Stria and Farin. She smiled as she thought of her old friends. Reyleen, or Rey as most called her, had her mother's dark skin and warrior heart, but she also had her father's quick brain and kind eyes.

It was the close friendship between her son and Rey that had given Tresstéanna the idea. Her son was too easy-going of late. He took his studies always with an ease and lack of focus that bothered her. Rey, on the other hand, had plenty of focus, and Tresstéanna hoped that Rey would have some to spare when it came to her son.

"Spoken by the woman who refused to use her own magic most of her life on the cliffs." Kriston snickered and shook his head, interrupting Tresstéanna's thoughts.

"You know why I couldn't," she said quickly in her own defense. She shook her head. "But, yes, as Té I should have studied my magic more."

For a time, they both thought back to when Tresstéanna had been split into three women, each with their own problems and difficult magic to control. Yet, despite the separation, all three had fallen in love with Kriston, and he had helped them regain their rightful form, together, which now sat next to him.

"Charlotte was on her way to the library, but she said the most interesting thing to me," Kriston muttered as he wrapped an arm around her. "She told me to stay close to you today."

Tresstéanna turned to look up at him. Concern bloomed until she saw him wink.

"My lady," came a stiff female voice from behind them. "My lord, Sir Seth is here."

"Thank you, Madeline. We will meet him in our private chambers," Tresstéanna replied. She gave Kriston's hand a gentle squeeze. "Time to go be queen and king."

1

THE ROYAL FAMILY

Reyleen Brelanna, captain of the Royal Air Guard, was furious. As she marched along the long, glorious hallways of Castle Pines anger bubbled inside her.

Reyleen, or Rey to her friends, was the youngest daughter of Stria and Farin. Her parents were close friends of the queen and king, friends who had traveled down inside the Kylix years ago with the band who had traveled to the other land called Midzark.

Rey, who was a dragon warrior holding a high level of six, was assigned to be the personal air guard of the royals while flying on their dragons. At least, she was trying to be. It appeared the prince had other plans.

Her long leather-clad legs ate up the distance quickly, but her prey was nowhere in sight. She wore her orange tank shirt, and her bare arms swung back and forth while she walked. Her deep brown eyes scanned the walkways and rooms she passed as she fisted her hands. She looked out the window at the castle's clock tower, located on the most western wall, and gritted her teeth.

"Eight fifty. Half the hour passed and didn't bother to show up," she hissed as she turned to continue her pursuit.

The castle's high ceilings and marble floors sent the sound of her boots echoing along the vast corridors. Beautifully made tapestries lined the walkways that wove around the royals' large home and several rugs were laid about the stone floors.

She felt her cheeks go heated with anger as she continued her search. Today, her long black hair was tied in the typical warrior's braids, and she felt the main braid swing against her back as she marched. Her brown leather riding gear creaked when she quickly stopped to look into one of the training rooms, hopeful her quarry was inside.

He wasn't here either! She quickly spun on her heels to continue her hunt. She usually enjoyed the hallways of the castle's training yards. Most days she took time to stop and talk with fellow warriors, dragon riders, and royal guards alike. But today she was on a mission.

"Where is that blasted man?" she hissed as she turned a corner. She almost ran over the young princess Charlotte, who had her arms full of books.

"Oh!" Charlotte said, her bright blue eyes wide with humor as Reyleen reached out quickly and helped the girl retain her balance. Charlotte had long dark hair like her father's, which was pulled into two braids on either side of her young round face. A thin silver crown breached her brow. Reyleen knew the young princess was six years younger than she, but whenever she looked into her blue eyes, she seemed older than her seventeen years.

"Sorry, Your Majesty, I didn't see you," Reyleen stated as she retracted her hand from Charlotte's pressed sleeve. She was sure her hands were still dirty from her earlier ride, and she didn't want to spoil the girl's pretty gray dress.

"That's okay, Rey," Charlotte said with a smile as she studied her with those odd clear eyes. "What bothers you today?"

After taking a deep breath, Rey wrinkled her nose and shook her head. "I'll give you one guess."

"Ah, my brother." Charlotte gave a quick smile, which faded quickly. "Oh, what happened to your arm?"

Charlotte's question had Rey glancing at her left arm, where a jagged red slash lay. The accident was one of the main reasons Reyleen was so on edge. She still felt the sting of injury caused when her knife had slipped while sharpening it the night before, but the missing prince was what had pushed the dragon warrior over the edge.

"Stupidity and rushing," Rey answered with a sigh. "No, it's fine," she stated as Charlotte moved to inspect it. "It will heal quickly enough. But I must really find your brother now." She gave a quick bow in Charlotte's direction and then sidestepped around her. She started back down the long hallway, intending to continue her search.

"Rey." Charlotte's call had her stopping and turning back to study the girl. "I know you're in a hurry, but I have something for you."

Rey looked back at the princess for a second. "For me?"

"Yes," Charlotte answered.

As Rey walked back to the princess, Charlotte took a small package from one of her dress's deep pockets. The package was wrapped in brown paper and was no bigger than the palm of her hand.

"I was going to give it to you on your birthday, but I think you should take it with you now," Charlotte stated with a shake of her head. "You don't have to open it now. In fact, I think you should wait. You will know when, but, well, happy birthday."

Rey had never heard the girl stutter before nor be at a loss for words. As the package was unceremoniously thrust into her hands, she watched in confusion as Charlotte took a deep breath and quickly spun on her heels then raced down the hallway. Charlotte never seemed to forget her birthday, which was still three days away. Rey wasn't shocked by the princess's gift; however, she was confused when the princess stopped and turned back.

"I think I saw Zander with Belent in the training yard," Charlotte said. She quickly turned and continued down the hallway at a run.

As Rey watched, the princess did something even more unusual. As Charlotte continued to race down the hall, she dropped her books on the stone floor and started to untie her long braids while she ran. Within a few steps, the girl's long dark hair waved behind her. She picked up her skirts and continued down the hallway at a faster pace, as if she was being chased.

When Princess Charlotte had finally disappeared, Rey shrugged her shoulders and shoved the package into her shoulder pack, then continued her hunt for the missing prince.

The anger had subsided a little when she finally found Prince Zander where his sister had said he would be, the training yard. The yard was currently full of warriors dodging and weaving in training practice. All except Zander and Sorcerer Belent.

Zander stood in the middle of the yard with his long legs firmly planted in a wide stance. His broad chest was thrust out in defiance, and the thin sorcerer circled him. He wore his gray military uniform, dark gray pants, and a light shirt, minus his overcoat. His dragon warrior patches were on the sash across his chest above a black leather belt that matched his boots.

Zander had a broad smile on his handsome face, and his light green eyes twinkled with amusement. The sun had tanned his high cheek bones and illuminated the fine almost-white strands that mixed in with the blond. A few pale blond strands waved in the breeze as he stood there in the yard.

"Come at me then," Zander taunted, waving one of his hands at Belent. Rey saw the cleft in his chin widen as he gave the sorcerer a broad smile.

"Taunting your enemy usually gets you nothing but pain," Belent hissed as the sorcerer continued to move around the prince. Belent was thin and tall. His once-brown hair was now speckled with gray at his temples, and lines creased around his brown eyes, giving him a distinguished look. His brown uniform spoke of his position in the queen's court, but the leather belt and satchel around his chest held no weapons.

"It might make them rush me, which could cause them to make a ... oof." Zander's last words were cut off when a large air bubble blew into the back of his legs, successfully throwing him off balance.

As she watched, she hated to acknowledge the joy she felt in seeing the prince land face first in the yard's dusty ground. But the smile had no sooner crossed her lips when her mouth fell open in awe. Prince Zander hadn't landed in the dirt but had rolled over the ground and, before she knew it, he quickly flipped backwards and was once again facing the sorcerer.

"Good, but I should not have been able to dislodge you at all," Belent shouted, once more circling Zander.

"You just caught me off my guard," Zander said as he once more planted his feet wide.

"Try harder," Belent urged as Rey approached the two men.

"I want to see you knock him down again," she insisted as she stood in front of Zander, mirroring his stance. "In fact, I can help you!" She smirked.

"Do you want to have a go at me, little lady?" Zander teased, clearly distracted by her appearance.

"Hmph," Rey said, ignoring his teasing manner. She shook her head. "You are late."

"Late?" Zander asked as he continued to look down at her, his soft green eyes still full of humor but also a little confusion. "For what?"

"Belent, would you please remind his royal pain in my highness that each Gunya day he has dragon training with me? And since the high council saw fit to place me in charge of his protection while on his dragon only twenty days ago, he has missed two lessons." She crossed her arms over her chest.

"Training?" Zander said with a frown. "Why do I need training on my dragon? I've been riding since I was six." He used the familiar contractions his mother had brought from Earth and taught her children. He shook his head and also crossed his arms, mirroring her stance now.

Quickly stepping closer and poking him once in his massive chest, she squinted her eyes at him. "Do I need to remind you of how I was able to knock you off Bree Nu twice only three days ago?"

"That? That was only because you caught me by surprise," Zander replied with a small laugh.

"Ah, much like Belent caught you by surprise a minute

ago." She took satisfaction in watching the grin fade from his handsome face.

"I think Reyleen has a point," Belent said quietly as he stood and stared at the two from a few feet away. "Sorry, I did not know he was expected in the dragon yard."

"It isn't your fault," Rey replied, also using contractions, which Zander had taught her when she was little. She turned to smile at Belent. "One does *not* expect greatness from someone who isn't fully trained yet." The snide comment only made Zander chuckle, causing her to glare at him.

"Your Majesty!" A green clad runner came up and handed Zander a parchment. He bowed and quickly left again.

Showing confusion on his face, Zander opened the roll and, after reading for a few seconds, turned to Belent.

"Trouble on the Eastern front," he told the sorcerer, quickly handing Belent the notice.

"Hm, looks like the pass is blocked. We may need to take a small regiment up there," Belent stated as Rey stepped closer.

"Is it the mists again?" she asked as she tried to read the notice.

"Yes," Zander said with a shake of his head. "I'll go tell Father. Can you get a small battalion ready?" he asked.

"I'm going with you." Belent's statement had Zander turning back to study the sorcerer. "Don't fight me on this. I mean to come."

With a nod to Belent, Zander turned and marched off to speak with his father, leaving Rey to gather a group of warriors to accompany them into the unknown.

The red mists, Zander thought with frustration as he turned away from Rey and Belent and marched out of the training yard.

The 'mist' as it was called by most in Genoa's army, was a menacing red haze that kept settling in odd places inside Genoa. Usually a fine mist wasn't concerning, but this one caused utter chaos wherever it appeared.

In some cases where the red haze settled, only the cattle were lost. However, six weeks ago they had a report from Parian that the haze had killed two families on the outskirts of that small town. The town was only four days north of Castle Pines. No other explanation had been found for the deaths of the eight people, raising the alarm as far south as the Maylin River.

Worry filled Zander as he quickly marched down the hallways of his home. Well, one of his homes. He had been raised in Castle Pines most of his childhood. The castle was settled on the lower side of Mount Lehar above the town of Pinewoods. He had grown up running through the woods, learning how to fight using sticks as swords, playing in the open plains, and riding his orange horse, Spirit.

He had also been raised far east along the Alluvion Ocean in the Draydon tribes' village on the edge of the Cliffs of Faro. That is where he felt more at home. He loved riding his dragon, Bree Nu, along the cliffs and feeling the spray of ocean water hit his face. He also loved learning the dragon warriors' ways. He was disappointed he only held a level three in the warrior tribe, but his royal duties kept him away from the coast most of the year.

He'd also spent some of his years in Valorna, the northern healing city that was settled on the shores of the Golden Enry lake. Time there was spent learning about the healing ways and Genoa's history. But his family resided most of the year in Castle Pines, which meant he too lived here, for he and his family were close.

His mother, the queen, kept busy ensuring her kingdom's peace, while his father helped maintain the land's army. Which wasn't to say his mother couldn't do her own fighting. She was known to still go out in the training yard and do some sparring every week. But now she mostly left the running of the army to his dad, Kriston.

Zander's two sisters also maintained a residence in Castle Pines. Caylee Shiarra, his twin, was as different from him as the moons were to each other. She was dark haired and had dark green eyes like their father. She was small of build and passionate about everything, but especially animals because, as she was quick to remind him, "They love without limitations."

Caylee also tended to boss Zander about. He assumed this was since she was seven minutes older, a fact she liked to remind him of whenever they argued or disagreed about something. But mostly he ignored her attempts to command him and did what he pleased.

Charlotte Marybeth, his younger sister by four years, had a demeanor more similar to Zander's. She had their father's dark hair but their mother's blue eyes. Charlotte loved books. She was seldom seen outside the great library, nor anywhere, without a book in her hands.

Caylee loved to ride her dragon Pin O, but she hadn't taken any of the dragon warrior lessons, as she preferred to stick to the ground and the libraries of Genoa.

His parents, however, loved to wander the lands they

ruled. Once a year, they would visit either the coast or Valorna, usually traveling there by way of their dragons.

As he turned towards the throne room, Zander continued to ponder the mystery of the mists. He was so deep in thought that he didn't hear the raised voices until it was too late.

"I tell you, they are nowhere to be found!" Uncle Seth's voice wasn't what made Zander hesitate. He enjoyed Seth, despite him not being an actual relation. He and his sisters had given Seth the nickname when they were very young, and it had stuck. No, it wasn't Seth's voice but the one that replied that gave him pause.

"Well, she cannot be bothered right now about that." Grant Worthington's voice caused the hairs on the back of Zander's neck to stand on end as he entered the antechamber to the throne room.

Zander didn't know why he reacted negatively each time he heard the man's voice, but the high tones always set him on edge. He saw Seth standing a few feet away from the other man, the two of them as different as could be. Seth had his arms, which were covered with warrior tattoos, crossed over his massive chest, and had a frown on his broad face. To Zander's amusement, his left foot tapped the floor in annoyance.

Grant, smaller than Seth by a whole foot, stood calmly blocking the large door into the throne room. His dark green eyes squinted as he stared at the warrior. Grant's eyes reminded Zander of a pond filled with decaying scum, probably because there was a mixture of mud brown along their odd green edges.

Someone had once made a comment to Zander that Grant was a pale likeness of him, with his blond hair, but the prince didn't think so. First, Zander's chin was stronger.

Yes, they both had a dimple at the end, but his own jawline was stronger. Also, he didn't have such a high forehead as Grant, who was possibly already fighting with a receding hairline.

Then there was the fact that Zander was at least two feet taller than Grant. Zander supposed the young man was handsome. His sister Caylee thought so, anyway, and Grant was currently courting his twin. Grant was usually dressed in the latest fashion but had fewer muscles than a true warrior should, according to Zander. And then there was his voice, which was a bit too whiny for Zander's liking.

"Bothered!" Seth bellowed as Zander drew near. "Her own parents are missing!"

"Missing?" Zander interjected as he quickly approached the two. "What do you mean, missing?"

As Seth turned to Zander, the young prince thought he saw relief in his face. "Finally. I've been trying to tell this cat's rear end of a man that the queen and king are missing, but he won't let me in to see Caylee or the advisors."

"Missing?" Zander mumbled. He pushed his way past Grant and opened the doors without a backwards glance at the two.

Caylee, his twin, was sitting on her own throne, one of three smaller chairs that were on the left side of the two high thrones. She glanced up as he entered, her dark brows drawn down in concentration. Her long dark brown hair was piled into many twists and braids today and a silver and golden crown encircled the thick locks. She wore a dress of dark blue; light golden lace encircled her tiny wrists while silver and gold glinted at her ears and fingers. Her dark green eyes studied him, and her brows raised in curiosity.

The three royal advisors who hovered around her chair turned as he entered. Zander saw a large map settled on his sister's lap, and several parchments littered the area near her feet.

"Morning," Zander said with a nod to Counselor Ray, a dear old friend of his father's who now was on the council to the queen and king. The other two advisors were either Blake and Fielder, or Blake and Feeder. Zander could never get the silver-haired man's name right, so he always called him sir.

"Brother," Caylee stated as he drew near. "We are in council at the moment."

Zander could hear annoyance in his sister's voice but turned and addressed Counselor Ray first. "I have just been advised by Seth that mother and father are missing." Zander saw shock on the man's face and turned to look at Seth. "Please tell us."

"It is true. I had just left their private council room and forgot my pack. When I returned into the room to gather it, they were both gone," Seth stated, concern written all over his face. "Ray, I smelled magic."

"Magic?" Ray reached up and brushed his fingers across his mustache. "Where is Belent?"

"I left him in the training yard. He is helping Rey gather a battalion. We have had news from the pass."

Ray's fingers continued to brush his upper lip as he listened about the newest report. When Caylee stood, Zander walked over and placed his hand on her arm.

"Don't panic. We don't yet know what the mist is, but it's my intent to go find out," he told her. He grew frustrated when Grant came and pulled her from him and gave her a hug.

"Darling, don't worry about that. I'm sure the prince has things well in hand." Grant stroked Caylee's back. "Go. I'm sure you can take care of the pass most efficiently."

Zander narrowed his eyes at the tone of command in the man's voice. But he didn't want to get tangled in another fight with Caylee about her choice in men, so he turned to Seth.

"Seth, please find Belent and have him meet us outside my parents' chamber." After nodding to the other two advisors, he and Counselor Ray left the room to look for his parents.

Before they reached the room, Zander stopped two guards and asked them to start a castle-wide search for his parents.

"No need to panic if they just slipped past Seth for a quiet moment," he told Ray as they entered the room in question.

"Would not be the first time," Ray mumbled, but he stopped just inside the doorway as the foul smell of magic hit him.

"Can you feel that?" Zander asked. He raised his hands and saw the very air turn blood red as it started to weave about his fingers.

"And smell it too," Ray said as Belent came up behind them.

"Out!" Belent hissed to them. He grabbed the two by their shirt collars and actually pulled them from the room. "There is dangerous magic in there," he warned as he quickly put himself between the two and the room. The red mist that now filled the chamber spun as if an invisible breeze stirred it.

"See, I too felt it," Seth said as he came quickly up to where the group stood in the hallway. "What is it?"

All eyes turned to Belent, who shook his head. He closed his eyes for a moment and the other three remained silent as the sorcerer stood stock still, his fingers barely reaching into the open doorway.

When he finally turned, his eyes were still closed but his face had gone pale. Giving his head another shake, he opened his eyes, and Zander noticed that his brown eyes were dilated and fixed. When the mist drew close to the doorway, Belent quickly shut the door and put a protective spell on it.

"Dark magic, darker than any I have ever felt. But one thing I do know—this room is no longer of Genoa."

The trap was set.

The all-powerful sorceress Io Maltesea stood in the clearing surrounded by darkness and double-checked her electrified net. She raised her long slender arms above her cloaked head, and she felt the net's power fade slightly then disappear completely. A wicked smile spread on her deformed lips as her eyes glowed red in the blackness.

No one in Genoa would feel the presence of her trap, until it was too late.

The smile fell quickly from her face, and she lowered her arms to her side. The cloak hid her features well, but nothing could mask her disfigurement as she slunk away from the spot and returned to the Lanart, a large wolf monster. The creature growled as she neared but then settled again when her magic crackled in its direction. She knew the creature wanted to snap at her with its sharp teeth, to tear her apart, but her powers held it back and kept it in her control.

After sitting on the Lanart's hairy back, she turned and studied her surroundings once more. She knew this place well. It had held much magic in the past, magic that still sizzled in the air. Magic that should be hers. But she was patient and knew there was an order to things.

First, she had to set her minion on the throne of Genoa. Then she could start her true scheme—total destruction of Genoa.

Giving the glade one last glance, she turned the Lanart around and used her sharp heels to kick it into action. It ran swiftly away from the tall broken stones and right into her red mist, away from her trap and back to her prison.

2

THE PATH TAKEN

Zander's frustration built as he sat on his throne and listened to the gathered royal advisors shout at each other.

There were several advisors from the southern territory, including two wind willows and a land sprite. The tree sprites remained stationary, but the gnomes stomped around, listening and occasionally shouting their own advice in their loud booming voices.

He always found the royal court tedious. Usually, the day-to-day ruling of the kingdom was done by his mother or his sister Caylee. He had neither the patience nor conviction to sit in a room every day and listen to the council whine and complain.

Zander was a man of action. He loved movement itself, the freedom to do as he pleased, when he pleased. Most of his days were spent in the training yards or out on patrols. Heck, he even didn't mind doing guard duty if it kept him out of doors.

He didn't mind when his royal duties called for him to take part in formal functions; he liked a good party. His favorite was when they traveled, either to Valorna or far south to Matera.

Zander wished he could go to Midzark, but his mother was adamant about restricting him to Genoa's mainland. He yearned to see the vast homeland of the giants, to see the Mellifera, the large bees that lived there. He tried to imagine the vast desert and the city of the Húriya people, Kós Kóvar, but only could imagine visions from Genoa.

He loved his home, loved the vast expansion of the Highman Plains, their colorful grasses and rolling hills filled with wild crystal-haired horses. All of the rivers and forests were dear to him. He particularly enjoyed his time along the ocean's edge. The Cliffs of Faro, where the dragons roosted and which the Draydon tribe called home, were where Zander felt the freest.

Now, sitting on his throne while he listened to the council members shouting, he had a fleeting thought of the faraway cliffs and freedom and sighed.

"We must enact law forty-two!" one advisor shouted as two more nodded their heads at this statement.

"There is no proof of death,' another shouted, and several others agreed.

"There have been plans in place for such an act," Counselor Ray said calmly, and Zander appreciated that the man didn't need to raise his voice to be heard by all gathered in the large room.

"No offense, but are the children ready to lead?" Counselor Blake demanded. His long hand reached up and touched his orange and yellow mustache as his odd orange eyes blinked. He was the only sand sprite to serve on the counsel, and as far as Zander knew, the only one in Castle Pines.

"Hey now!" Zander objected at being called a child. He

quieted, however, when he felt Caylee's small hand rest on his arm.

"Gentlemen," she said from her own throne to his right. "The discussion of who rules is not yet needed. We are here to decide where to look for the queen and king first."

"Begging your pardon, Your Highness, but even that decision must be made by one of authority," Counselor Blake replied.

"Then we will make it!" Zander interjected quickly as his temper rose again.

"Where is Charlotte?" Caylee asked softly to Seth, who stood to the left of the room.

"I was told they were unable to locate her." Seth's reply had Zander standing quickly.

"Not her too?" he asked. He headed towards the door, but Counselor Ray stopped him.

"No, you must remain here. I will have Seth and two guards search for her now." He patted Zander's shoulder.

"Probably somewhere in the library, hidden in a corner with a book," Seth mumbled, but Zander saw worry filling his face as he quickly left the room to search.

"Look, there are three of us to divide our parents' responsibilities," Caylee started. She held up a hand when Zander opened his mouth as he approached her and sat back down. "I know the mist blocking the pass needs to be inspected, but with the attack on our family, we must remain here, where it is safe," she pleaded.

"But here isn't safe," Zander quietly said, grabbing her arms. "I know the mist is connected; maybe I can find out who or what is causing this. And in discovering this, we might find where Mom and Dad are. Caylee, we know the mist is at the pass, right now."

He saw worry and fear in his sister's dark green eyes as

they sat there amongst the royal councilors. He saw the minute she understood he couldn't remain here, inactive, while their parents were out there, maybe trapped in the very mists that clogged the pass only a few miles away.

"What shall we do?" she asked him softly as the advisors continued to argue around them.

"What they raised us to do," Zander stated strongly. He gripped her small hand in his. "And what they themselves would do." The smile on his face was one of determination as he looked up at the counselor's faces staring back at them. "I will go to the pass and hunt down the red mists to find our parents."

"I will help you," Sorcerer Belent stated with conviction.

Zander gave his friend a nod and turned to look at Caylee. "Sister, Genoa counts on your wisdom to govern. I ask that you remain here, safe with the royal guard to protect you and Charlotte. When I find Mom and Dad, I will return them to us."

Caylee raised her pointed chin a little higher and then gave him a nod. Fear flashed in her eyes, but there was also determination, something Zander knew would carry her far, despite her misgivings.

"Very well but know this. If you do not return within ten days, I will depart to track you down." Her green eyes narrowed at him as if daring him to disagree with her statement.

"Understood," he said with a nod. "Belent, please tell Rey we will take a full regiment of men."

"Take Corbin and Sash with you," Caylee pleaded as she grabbed his arm to prevent him from turning immediately from her.

"And Seth," Zander agreed with a smile, "for entertainment." He smiled down at his sister but saw beyond her worry. "As soon as possible, send word to Wizard Col and Timmons, maybe even to cousin Calob in Matera. Heck, might as well tell all the others too. They will come." He knew his sister understood that he meant all their allies, including the dragon tribes and even the king of Malic.

She nodded at his words as he turned to leave.

He changed into his riding clothes—black pants and a blue shirt with leather chest straps that kept him on the dragon. Before he had finished saddling Bree Nu, his bright blue and black dragon, word had reached him that Charlotte had not been found in the castle.

"Then we hunt for her as well," Zander said, and with conviction he swiftly climbed on his dragon's back. Thirty warriors also mounted their dragons behind him in the dragon training yard. Rey, Seth, and Belent were nearest him, along with his best friend Corbin, whose bright red hair shone bright in the noon sun.

Corbin Timmons had always been Zander's closest friend, much like their fathers still were. Corbin was built like his father but had the bright hair of his mother, as did his three sisters. The senior Timmons was off in the west at the moment, otherwise Zander was sure he too would have joined the hunt.

The heat of the day had just reached its peak above Castle Pines and the clock tower showed that it was a few minutes before ten, the middle of the day for Genoa. The large band circled in the air once and set off for the edge of the Helmand Mountains. The plan was to quickly reach the glade along the old outlook, which was nestled in a large, open field at the bottom of the pass. There, they would leave their dragons and go on foot. If they were lucky, they would reach their destination well before dark.

Zander studied the woods far below Bree Nu's blue wings and thought of his parents. In his mind's eyes he saw his beautiful mother smiling at him, her soft blond hair curling about her face. He remembered the stories she told of her adventures before coming to Genoa and of her struggles in the prevention of the destruction of Genoa, which he jokingly called the "non-war." His favorites, of course, were the stories of the giants and their homeland, Midzark, because he knew most of the giants from her tales. They regularly traveled to the mainland and stayed in a quaint yet very large cottage that had been built for them just outside of Castle Pines.

He thought of his father next, how he had taught Zander how to wield a sword, to ride bareback on his horse, and how to survive out in their world. To Zander, his father was one of the best warriors, only matched by his mother, of course.

This thought brought a smile to his lips, and he realized that no matter where his parents were, they were together and probably taking care of each other. His smile only faltered when he thought of his younger sister, Charlotte.

Charlotte was only seventeen. This thought filled him with fear for her. Yes, most of the time she seemed wiser and older than he or Caylee. She was always settling arguments between the twins. Most of the time it was she, the youngest, who reminded them of their duties. Yet she was so small and alone.

He had been told that no red mist had filled Charlotte's room, which had given him hope, but more worries filled his mind. She could have been killed right away, but then her body would have been discovered. He had to remind himself of this fact several times. Then the thought of her being kidnapped came to him. Would there be a ransom demand?

Shaking his head hard, he looked down and realized he had almost flown over the outlook.

"Have faith," Bree Nu said as he banked the dragon towards the ground. "Your family is strong."

Nodding, he watched the ground draw closer and took comfort in the dragon's words. "We will find them. We must."

Two men from his group were left at the outlook to look after the dragons, as the patrol that was stationed there already had a full duty roster. This meant the number of their group dropped to twenty-eight, but Zander felt that having a sorcerer in the group, along with the giant warrior Sash, more than made up for the missing two.

"Tell me again," Corbin demanded as he walked next to Zander. Both had their broad swords hitched across their backs, but Corbin's hung with the handle above his right shoulder instead of his left. His features were like Zander's, except he had the skin tone of a true redhead, thanks to his mom, Rayshell.

Zander squinted his eyes up as they followed the well-worn path leading up into the pass. It led to where the stones had once resided years before. "The room was filled with red mist."

"No, you said it filled with the mist after Belent got there."

"Actually, I think it was after you reached out to touch the air," Seth provided from behind the two.

"He touched the air and then it turned red?" Corbin asked.

"You think the mist would have taken the prince as

well?" Rey asked from in front of them, her dark eyes continuously scanned the woods for danger.

"I don't know," Corbin said as he scratched his head. "I think it's odd that Seth didn't see the mists and neither did Counselor Rey or Zander until after he entered the room."

"It was not there when I went back for my bag," Seth confirmed, and Zander saw him scan the woods.

"Maybe Belent should have stayed with Caylee," Zander mumbled as concern for his twin started to grow again.

"No, I am needed here," Belent stated as he joined Zander on the path. He then placed a hand on Zander's arm and nodded. "She is being protected by Captain Adams."

"I just wish Wizards Leian and Shiarra were back in Castle Pines," Zander said with a sigh.

"Yes, I too would feel better if we had left a wizard behind for your sister, but since Cenzic passed, and Col is east with the tribe, that only left me." Belent replied.

"I didn't mean you weren't enough; it's just I worry for her," Zander said. He stopped walking and placed a hand on the man's shoulder. "I know you have protected my family well, but we are now scattered and—"

"I understand," Belent interjected and nodded his thin face. "But now that Captain Adams is aware of the danger, he and his men will protect Caylee as if she were the queen."

Nodding, Zander started walking again.

Three hours before the sun would set in the east, Zander and his band of warriors reached the bank of trees that encircled the odd meadow that had once held the entombed kings of old in their stone prisons. Now broken, the massive stones littered the area, leaving only a circle of wreckage.

"Be on the lookout. The report said the mists could be seen from here," Zander warned as they neared the start of the meadow.

"I feel nothing out of place here," Belent said, his dark brows drawn together as his dark eyes narrowed in concentration. "Nor do I see any mist."

"Stay together," Rey demanded. She was the first one to slowly walk out of the safety of the trees and into the meadow. Her riding leathers were the only sound for a second before she drew her swords, two sharp short blades that shone in the failing light.

Belent quickly followed and then the others, each drawing their weapons. Zander was unceremoniously shoved backwards by Sash. The giant bald man still had muscles bigger than a dragon, and with his broad swords drawn, Zander didn't want to argue with him. But when Seth tried to push in front of him, he drew the line.

"Hey now," he hissed, only to be shushed by the dragon warrior. Remembering Seth held a higher level than he, Zander waited until five more high-ranking warriors passed him before finally continuing forward. The remaining dragon warriors closed in ranks behind him.

"There's a foul smell here," Rey said as she reached the remains of the first stone. Her dark eyes scanned their surroundings, and her body was tense. Zander saw her arm muscles flex once as she twisted and held her blades up.

"It could be remnants of what was once here," Belent

said as he stopped and turned on the spot, his arms outstretched as if feeling for danger in the air.

As Zander drew near, he felt a sizzling sensation in the air. He raised his free hand, much like he had done in his parents' chamber, and his eyes grew wide as a red mist suddenly appeared before him out of thin air.

"Get back!" Belent shouted as Zander's vision dimmed and his ears filled with a loud popping noise.

"Ugh! Fall back!" he heard Rey shout from somewhere to his left.

"This way!" a voice shouted.

"No!" Belent shouted, and Zander saw a great white flash before he was thrown to the ground. He hit the ground hard on his right shoulder and felt all of the rocks beneath him. His head swam and his ears buzzed.

"What—?" He had to stop and clear his throat which felt hot and scorched, then he tried to speak again. "What was that?"

"That, dude, was awesome!" came an unfamiliar voice.

"Are you all performers?" a woman asked. Zander blinked quickly and stared up into a bright blinding light above his head.

Suddenly, a blast of confusing noises and lights seemed to surround him, and then he felt Sash pull him up. Standing, he glanced around and tried to make sense of what he was seeing and hearing. All of his senses were being bombarded by the unknown, or unexpected.

He no longer stood in a forest meadow deep in the Helmand Mountains. Instead, he was in a vast city, surrounded by buildings and encircled by several strange people. Sash, Seth, and Belent drew close to him. Rey was standing guard; she had sheathed her swords and was trying to push back anyone who tried to get near him. He glanced at the other dragon warriors, though not all of them were there. He counted a total of eleven from his group currently surrounding him.

Rey, Belent, Sash, and Seth were closest, but Kenso, Avaline, Kylo, and Mateo, who were all higher ranks than him, along with Mika and Leon, who were of lower ranks, all still had their weapons raised at the surrounding crowd. He didn't see any of the others that had been at the stones with him, and concern for his missing friends mixed in with his confusion.

"Is this supposed to be a magic show?" a stranger asked, and Zander realized he had been the one who had called him 'dude.'

Beyond his fellow warriors, Zander saw something that had his blood running cold in his veins. Beyond and above towered the tallest buildings Zander had ever seen in his life. Black and red bricked buildings rose well beyond his head and reached far into the darkened sky above them. Several contained square lights lined up in rows that raced up the structure's sides and gave him a dizzy sensation until they disappeared into the darkness of night.

Steam rose from vents in round rocks below his feet, and the stench of cooked foods mixed with the smell of sewage filled his nostrils. The noise of his surroundings also blasted him. Horns blared, music boomed, and the sound of thousands of people talking bounced off the tall walls.

"I think they are from the tae kwon do place down the street," a woman speculated as Zander continued to stare about in a daze.

"Cats. We're on Earth," he finally hissed. Belent turned and looked at him. The sorcerer's face went pale with his words, but after a second, he nodded.

"Earth." Belent slowly turned to Seth. "Seth, we have to—"

"I know," Seth interrupted. He sheathed his sword and immediately stepped to Rey, who was trying to push the crowd back. "Listen," he said as he grabbed her arm and lowered his voice to a whisper. "Distractions are needed. Run drills."

Zander saw confusion cross Rey's pretty face, but then she nodded once and gave a short, sharp whistle, which caused the dragon warriors to fall into line.

"Gather and watch the finest warriors of all give you a little demonstration," Seth shouted as he pushed Zander aside so that Rey could lead the warriors in their slow dance of warm-up drills.

Zander, still struck by the fact that he and his friends now stood on Earth, continued to stare at the massive buildings with his mouth hanging open. The sights and smells and sounds were almost too much to take in and left him feeling dizzy as he tried to look at everything.

He saw people milling about, some quickly walking and others sitting in chairs or on the hard stone floor. Fast-moving wheeled machines of all sizes lumbered down the streets, crisscrossing the area on roads. These must be the cars his mother had told him about. Lights flashed everywhere. Reds, yellows, and greens blinked names and directions, causing a small headache to form behind his left eye.

Rey had the dragon warriors do a slow-motion performance for the gathered audience, which pressed in closer. Swords were now sheathed as each warrior swayed and dipped in their exercises. Arms lifted and muscles flashed as they gave an impressive performance of the 'Dragon Rise' exercise. She then smoothly led them into the 'Sea Serpent' drill. Her face was flushed, but Zander saw that her eyes continued to scan the area, always looking out for dangers.

"Your mother's warnings of this place must be heeded. We cannot let them know we hold magic or are from Genoa," Belent whispered in his ear, distracting him from his surroundings. "What do you know of this place?"

Shaking his head, Zander thought back to all the stories his mother had told him. Earth. Cats, he was on Earth. He remembered her warnings. Her struggles living on Earth had been numerous. She had spent years here running and hiding from the government of this place. She had lived alone, never knowing her true origins or who she really was.

Stories quickly flashed in his mind of some of her struggles. She had told of living on the streets, hiding in dark alleys, always just a step ahead of the hated General Wilberg and his men. Yet she had also told of wonders of Earth, such as cars, planes, and other comforts, some of which she had tried to recreate in Genoa. Medicines and plumbing were only part of what Anna had brought from Earth, yet other things she had left out.

But Zander loved the stories she told her children of the adventure of travel the most. She had spoken of vast forests where the red trees are taller than any found on Genoa. Of hot deserts and wet plains, of vast mountains and large rivers.

Turning, he studied their surroundings once again and tried to think of the cities his mother had told him about. When nothing came to his mind, he turned to look back at Belent and shook his head.

"We have to find out which city we're in first," Zander finally said.

Belent gave a nod and left his side to move out amongst the crowd. Zander saw him move about the crowd with his brown, floppy hat held out. Seth and Sash moved to stand beside him in a protective stance as Belent continued to weave in and out of the gathered crowd.

Confused at first, Zander watched as person after person placed coins into the sorcerer's hat. Then he saw Belent wave his hand over a woman's head and saw a blank look cross her face for a second. Then she too emptied her pockets and dropped several pieces of paper into the sorcerer's hat.

Over and over again the sorcerer did this until the hat was quite full of currency. The crowd loudly applauded several times as Rey continued to lead the drills, much to the pleasure of the onlookers. Soon, several of the warriors were doing flips and spins in a free format drill.

When Belent finally returned to Zander's side, he whispered one word to Zander.

"Denver."

3

DENVER OR BUST

Rey grew frustrated when the crowd around her people didn't disperse like she had hoped. Instead, the drills she and her people ran seemed to bring even more onlookers. As they drew nearer, her warrior instincts took over and she wanted to draw her swords again.

She noticed that Zander and the sorcerer, Belent, were in tight counsel after he had returned from walking amongst the crowd. She thought he or Zander would come over and explain something soon, but they continued to speak together in quiet tones and her frustration built.

Seth and Sash drew closer, and she ground her teeth when both nodded their heads at her and, without saying anything, took off in opposite directions. Belent turned and handed Zander his filled hat, and the prince immediately started to sort the hat's contents while the sorcerer once again walked amongst the crowd.

"What are they doing?" she hissed. She turned back to her company and had them start one more drill, her favorite, the 'Twisting Queen.' It consisted of dips and turns, and at the end had her bounding into the midst of the spinning warriors and doing an impressive round kick.

After the final kick was finished, they bowed to the crowd and received an exceptionally long applause. Several coins were thrown their way and she looked up to see Zander smiling in her direction. His eyes sparkled, and she had a fleeting impression that he considered this whole affair an adventure.

After giving her warriors a quick nod as a signal, they took up a defensive circle around the prince once again. She slowly approached Zander, who immediately held up his hand, asking her to wait a moment as several strangers came close to talk to them.

"Wow! That was awesome!" a man shouted, his brown eyes on her as he gave her a wide smile. "Say, are you free to grab a drink with me and my friend?" She squinted her eyes at him in distrust.

"I'm sorry, the lady isn't available right now; we have another performance," Zander said as he placed a hand on her shoulder. Normally she would have punched anyone who tried to get fresh with her, but Zander was her crown prince, so she turned her eyes on him in question. "Thanks for watching," he added with a wink in her direction and gave the men a broad smile.

"I think you just broke their hearts," Seth said as he approached them. "I found what we are looking for two streets this way," he said as Belent returned carrying another hat full of currency.

"How much?" the sorcerer asked.

"I could be wrong, but most of these are ones. So far, we have about three hundred, but I don't know if staying out here is wise," Zander replied as he shook his head.

"Could we risk another show?" Belent asked the prince.

The two turned and looked around the street for a minute as Sash came back at a quick trot.

"Keepers three streets that way," the large man said as eyes turned in the direction he had pointed.

"I guess that's our answer," Belent replied as he waved the others closer. "We are in enemy territory. We cannot draw attention to ourselves. Cover your weapons and draw your hoods close, my friends. We need to split into two groups. Seth will lead the prince and four others, while I take the remaining. Zander, please use your skills and acquire us a place for the night."

It was at this moment that Rey realized the sun had set. She also felt a cool chill in the air, which promised of rain. The air felt different. Instead of the warmth of midsummer, it felt more like the bitter bite of harvest season.

"We will wait until you come out to collect us, but at no point are you to draw attention to yourselves or speak to anyone," Belent warned as he quickly handed his filled hat to Zander. "I just hope that's enough. Get two or three rooms if you can."

Zander nodded once and then they were moving. She walked next to the prince, who was closely followed by Corbin and the warrior Avaline. Sash was on the other side of Zander, and as they moved, the large warrior took out his rain parka and covered his massive form with the leather coat. She too moved to remove her coat from her pack, but Zander had beat her to it.

"Here, let me help," he said with a smile. "We find ourselves on Earth, the planet my mom was exiled on," he explained as he helped her cover her weapons with her coat. "We are going to an inn where I will need to get a few rooms. However, I will need you to hold onto my broad sword while I go in," he said.

She shook her head. "No, you go nowhere without me." She frowned up at him. "You are under my protection; it is my job to ensure you are safe."

He sighed once and then quickly nodded. "Okay, but you will do as I say. Give your swords to Avaline or Corbin." He nodded once as his friend came close to them. "You can keep your small knives but hide them under your cloak," he supplied as she started to argue. "Trust me, we will be in no danger yet, as long as we don't draw attention to ourselves."

Knowing nothing about this Earth land, she quickly handed her swords to Avaline, who slipped them under her own cloak. Zander gave Corbin his massive broad sword and had just thrown his own cloak closed when they approached a tall building. Flashing lights of red and green assaulted the air above the wide triple doors, indicating the inn had available rooms along with several other amenities.

Seth, Zander, and she moved to enter the building while Corbin, Sash, and Avaline remained near the doorway, sticking to the darkness, away from the lights.

"Are you ready?" Seth asked Zander, who nodded once and squinted his eyes. Rey knew the look; it meant the prince was going to use his magic. This was something she loved about the royals, their inborn magic. It was also something she envied. She knew Charlotte used her magic with the books she coveted. She had asked the princess once to show her how she used her magic but had been disappointed when she had failed to see anything other than the girl touch the book and close her eyes. After a second or two, Charlotte had looked up and smiled, indicating she had finished, but Rey hadn't been able to see anything.

She knew Caylee also held magic but had never seen or known what form her magic took. Zander, on the other hand, showed his magic quite a bit, usually when he was goofing off with his friends. One time he had lost a sparring battle with Corbin and had turned his friend's warrior clothing into a fancy pink dress. The dress's color had clashed with the bright red hair but matched his angry cheeks. Corbin had tripped over the long hem and ended up on the floor. Zander had stood over him laughing, and soon Corbin had joined in the merriment.

She always found Zander's show of magic interesting, but she still wasn't prepared for what form his magic took now as they passed through the large glass doors.

Instead of her warrior clothing and her long cloak, she shockingly found herself in a very thin, very revealing black dress. Her strong arms were bare, as was her neck. The dress's neckline dipped low on her breasts, and she quickly noted that the bottom half of the dress was missing. The black material hit her mid-thigh and her sensible warrior boots had been magically replaced with stupidly high shoes.

"Dear lord," Zander hissed next to her as he placed a helping hand in the center of her back. "Don't trip in those," he whispered in her ear.

"Well then don't give them to me." She returned his hiss and saw that he too had a vision of different clothing covering him.

She knew the visions weren't real, as Zander's royal magic couldn't cause physical change. He couldn't change the way something looked forever but, much like a cloak did, he could draw a different image over something, as long as he focused.

He and Seth were currently wearing dark shirts and pants that were pressed and pleated. Black shoes that shone in the inn's bright lights replaced their dusty boots, and gold glinted on their wrists and fingers. She too had jewelry adorning her neck and arms, including a wedding ring on her left hand. She cocked an eyebrow at that and heard Zander softly chuckle at her assessment.

"Just an illusion my dear." His words had her clenching her teeth as they walked into the vast entrance of the hotel. The interior reminded her of the smaller guest entrances of Castle Pines. Large white beams held the ceiling aloft and bright lights reflected off black marble flooring. Everything looked new and shiny.

They approached a broad white desk with three people sitting behind it, two women and one pale man. Odd boxes were set before them, which they studied with great interest. She didn't know what they were, so she kept her eyes on Zander as they drew near.

"How may we help you?" the blond female asked with a large toothy grin aimed at them.

Rey noticed the woman glance briefly at her, then look at Zander. The woman's blue eyes widened, and her smile increased by a few inches.

He has that effect on all women, Rey thought as she too diverted her eyes back to Zander.

"Yes." Zander leaned closer to the blonde but kept his arm around Rey. "Missy," he said as he read the woman's name tag, which was set over her left breast. "My friends and I are going to need to acquire some rooms tonight."

"Ah yes, I can help you with that." Missy batted her long lashes at Zander. "How many rooms are you needing?"

"Well, here's the rub. I'm not sure how many of my friends are coming. I know we need at least three." He moved the hand from Rey's back and leaned forward to study Missy more closely. "But I'm not sure of your prices."

Rey saw Missy's cheeks turn pink as she gave a quote to Zander, who thought for a minute and turned to Seth.

"So, three rooms?" he asked. Seth gave a quick nod. "Yes, that should do us for tonight," Zander replied with a smile.

"Sure. Do you want them all near each other?" Missy asked as she turned her attention to the square lighted box in front of her.

"Yes, I should think so," Zander replied.

"I'll need an ID and credit card," Missy said sweetly.

"I'll be paying cash," Zander replied as he pulled out a small square leather container and handed the woman an odd-looking square object.

"Cash will do, Mr....?" Missy squinted at the object and then smiled broadly. "Mr. Bond."

"Who's Bond?" Rey asked as soon as they were in one of the private rooms Zander had acquired.

"What?" Zander asked her distractedly as he studied the vast room.

The room had two 'queen beds' according to Missy. Zander thought the name of the beds was funny but realized it had something to do with their size and not who would be sleeping in them. There were also two chairs, a table, and a large black square on one wall. The large bathroom was connected, and there was something called a mini fridge, which he discovered was a cold box.

"Oh, Bond?" he asked, as he bent down to study the fridge. "My mom told me about him. He's a spy."

"A spy? In Castle Pines?" Rey asked quickly. She tried

to draw her short knife, as if needing to defend herself from an imaginary person.

Chuckling, Zander stood up and studied her. She kept trying to grasp her knife but couldn't locate it under his magical spell. Her hand kept brushing along her right thigh in frustration until he finally laughed out loud.

"No, not in Genoa, here on Earth," he said as she stopped and narrowed her eyes at him.

"Take this illusion off me," she insisted as her left toe tapped against the ground in frustration.

He liked how pretty she looked when she was frustrated. Her dark skin shone in the single lamp and her toned arms and legs were nice to look at in the simple dress he had given her under his magical illusion. He had seen another woman wear something similar as they had walked to the inn and had immediately chosen it for Rey. The suits he and Seth now wore were from two men he had also spotted just outside the building. He thought they looked expensive and classy.

"I don't know, I kind of like that outfit on you," he teased as her eyes became dangerously narrow. "Don't you like that dress?"

"What dress? This isn't a dress, it's a slip!" she hissed, and tried to cover parts of herself with her hands.

"Your riding leathers show more skin than that thing." He laughed again as she quickly grabbed a pillow from the bed and launched it at him. "Okay, okay, I'll stop, but I think I should wait until Seth and the others are back. It's hard to undo one and not the others," he said with a smile.

He saw her nod once and then she moved to the wall of windows. It took her a second, then she figured out how to pull the drapes across the window, blocking out the city's vast nightline.

"Zander." She turned to study him. "How did we get here?"

He took a deep breath and thought about her question. How had they arrived on Earth?

As Anna, his mother had been banished to Earth, taken as a small child by a wizard who had helped her escape Zander's own grandfather, King Haddock. She had only been able to return to Genoa because Wizard Leian had come and fetched her. The wizard had used the Orick, a magical portal built of stones in Genoa.

He thought of Rey's questions and wondered if there had been magic left in the stones that had imprisoned the kings of old. Maybe the red mist had sparked the old magic?

"I don't know," he finally answered. "Maybe Belent will know more."

She nodded before walking over to listen at the door, her ear close to the dark wood. Her rear end stuck out towards him, giving him another nice vision.

"They should be here soon," she said. "Neat. There's this little peephole in the door."

"I think this door leads to the other rooms," Zander said as he turned away from her and opened a door on the side of the room. "Missy said they were connecting rooms."

"Good," Rey replied distractedly, and Zander gave her backside another long glance as she stood there looking out through the peephole.

Belent and the others finally joined them in the largest room. He tried not to laugh at Sash wearing a very large suit. When the warrior gave him a threatening look, he quickly pulled his magic back, so all his friends, along with everyone else, were once again wearing their Genoa clothing.

"That's better," Corbin said with a sigh.

"You didn't like the suit," Avaline asked him, and Zander saw her gray eyes twinkle at his best friend.

"It clashed with my hair," Corbin said with a grin, tugging a long blond lock of hers.

"If you two are finished, we have plans we need to discuss," Belent interjected with a hint of frustration.

"First. I think we should hear all what Zander knows about this place," Rey advised as she settled comfortably on one of the beds. Everyone quickly agreed with the dragon warrior, and they too settled about the room.

"Fine, but first, I'm starving. Does anyone have their food pouches?" he asked.

Corbin passed him a flat cake and after taking a large bite, he started telling them what little he knew about Earth.

"Mom said the military was vast. They communicate quickly with each other and have branches in each city. She had to go under the radar. I don't know what that means exactly, but she did this so she wouldn't be caught. I think it means she had to use disguises a lot. She dressed like a boy sometimes and would ride in train carts. They are like long wagons that run on steam or something," he quickly supplied when he received blank looks from everyone. "I know time is shorter here, so I personally hope that General Wilberg is dead."

"He hunted your mother, right?" Seth asked.

"Hunted and would have killed her," Zander said with a shake of his head. "And we can't draw attention to ourselves."

"That display we put on tonight might draw attention," Kenzo stated. He was a large mixed-raced man with dark skin and almond-shaped eyes who was a level below Rey. He was two years older than Zander and quite an impressive ax thrower. His red dragon tattoo would have drawn attention in any room, along with his mohawk and heavily pierced ears.

"Performers are in any city," Seth stated, trying to defend his quick decision to cover their abrupt entrance into this land.

"It was a good plan," Belent spoke up quickly. "Our arrival had already been spotted, and though magic isn't here on Earth, tricks can easily be explained to those who live here."

"Belent is correct," Zander said with a smile. "Mom told us that magic is usually mistaken for tricks here. She told of stories from this land where magic is wished for or even dreamed about."

"So, how do we get home?" Sash asked as all eyes turned to the large man.

"That, my dear friend, is a great question," Belent stated. He turned to Zander.

"I don't know." Zander stood to pace down the center of the room. "Leian took my mother home using the Orick, but that was in a town called Boston. He also had Fin Crystals with him." Here he looked over at Belent, who shook his head, indicating he didn't carry any of the rare crystals. "I didn't think you would have any," Zander said with a sigh.

"Are there any more magical portals here?" the warrior Kylo asked. He was a black man of Zander's own age; his gray dragon tattoo was hidden under his thick thatch of wavy hair. But he too had muscles to spare under his yellow-lined leathers.

Zander thought with all the dragon warriors inside one room, the room would feel small, but everyone had settled either on the floor, in the few chairs, or even on the beds. This gave him plenty of room to pace up and down on the soft carpet as he thought about the question.

"Mother spoke of a wardrobe, magical shoes, and a tornado, but I think those were just stories," Zander said with another shake of his head.

"Then what we need to do is find a library," Rey stated, standing up from the bed.

"Not at night," Zander said with a shake of his head. "I do know the nighttime is short and dangerous."

"Animals?" Avaline asked innocently.

Her question had them all thinking of the many wild animals that lived on their home world, but Zander quickly shook his head no.

"There are other things more dangerous than a cat." He turned to study the dark black square on the wall. "I think this is a TZ." He frowned as he thought. "No, a TV. Let me look." He found a button on the box and smiled and stood back when it came to life.

"Ah!" he exclaimed and bent down to study the small controller. "Yes, Mother told me about these. This can help us know more about Earth."

"How?" Rey asked as she stood quickly to study the image on the box. A man was showing a small metal tube and words flashed across the screen giving the product's name.

"There are people on here who will give news. It can also teach us what to expect here." He proceeded to hit several buttons, which changed the images on the screen.

"Let me try," Corbin said as he too stood and tried to grab the controller from Zander.

"The other rooms have this too," Seth stated.

"I'm going to try the one over here," Kylo said. He quickly stood and disappeared into the adjoining room.

"I want a try," Corbin said again as Zander continued to hit several buttons.

"Go get your own. I'm playing with this one." Zander blew out a quick breath of frustration, and Rey quickly grabbed the controller from his hands.

"Boys," she spat, "it's not a toy." She hit a button and found the news station. She shook her head at the two men, who stood there pouting when they realized they wouldn't get to play with the machine.

The news came on and, much to their confusion and dismay, it was filled with woes and dangers. Stories of faraway incidents scared them because they didn't know how close the countries were. Frequently, a map would be provided prior to a story, but worry still filled the group from Genoa.

"This place is a mess," Seth said with a shake of his head.

"There are many wars here," Rey said sadly.

"Mother said there are always wars. She said Earth has been in conflict for generations. What we need, however, is local news." Zander plopped down on the end of the bed as a series of commercials flashed on the screen.

"Ah, should I change the image?" Rey asked as she sat next to him.

"No, I think they said that is up next," Corbin answered as he continued to stand off to the side.

The local news came on, and they heard about traffic, construction plans, and sports, something all the men found interesting. A sport called football where the men wore helmets and strange uniforms had Zander itching to learn more.

When news of arrests and activities within Denver flashed on, they all breathed a sigh of relief that their little appearance didn't flash on the screen.

Zander was finally able to coax the controller from Rey and found a thrilling story full of action and adventure.

"I don't think this is true," Rey finally said as a man on the screen jumped out of a flying machine.

"No, but it's entertaining," Corbin said as he finally sat on the edge of the bed. Half of the warriors were now surrounding the two room's TVs. Kylo had found another story about great warriors from space, and half of their group moved between the rooms just to ensure they didn't miss any of the action on the screens.

"What we need," Belent said sharply, "is information about Denver."

"Yes, but for now, we can learn about Earth," Zander said as he leaned closer to the screen. "There will be plenty of time tomorrow to learn about Denver."

4

IDEAS ARE FOR IDIOTS

The first thing they learned about Denver was the nights were loud.

Eventually, they had all settled down for bed. Zander was used to sleeping in his private chambers at home, or even in the quiet forests east of his home. Here, he lay in the dark as the noise blared from outside. Apparently, Denver was a city where no one slept.

They were on the tenth floor of the hotel, but even so, the noise from the street far below carried up to their rooms. Sirens wailed periodically while car horns sounded. Laughter raced up the hotel's halls and right into their rooms.

"Doesn't anyone sleep here?" Corbin asked, and Zander heard his friend punch the small pillow once as the bed creaked underneath him. "Too loud here for even a gnome to fall asleep."

They had divided into the three rooms. The women—Rey, Avaline and Mika—took one room while the other two were split by the nine men. Zander, Corbin, Mateo, Kenzo, and Kylo all slept in one while Belent, Sash, Seth, and

Leon used the other. Of course, each room had only two large beds, so they fought for the soft mattresses. Kenzo had lost. The large man had only shrugged and thrown several pads from the chairs down to make a sleeping spot near the wall.

"I could always smother you with that pillow," Kenzo replied to Corbin's comment from his spot on the floor. "Then we would not hear you snore."

"I just hope Kylo does not talk in his sleep tonight," Mateo said. He was a pale man with unruly black hair and a wide grin. He held a dragon warrior level of four. His green dragon tattoo was mostly covered by his long hair, but he sported a rather risqué one on his forearm of a naked wood nymph.

The little clock on the table next to Zander's bed flashed 2:30 before Zander heard the city outside finally settle down. Kylo did talk and Corbin's snores were a soft muffled noise as he felt himself eventually drifting off to slumber.

"Brother."

Zander stirred in his sleep until the call came again.

"Brother."

Zander discovered himself standing at the edge of a cliff. Turning, he noticed his mother's golden dragon, Su Na, sat on the ledge next to him. The ocean spanned vast before him while the land dropped away hundreds of feet below. The yellow moon, Blinske, was high in the sky above the water. Grenata, the green dragon moon, skimmed the ocean's horizon to his left, telling him it was late afternoon, though he didn't know what day.

Unsure where along the coast he was, he looked up and down the shoreline but found no familiar landscapes. The rocks and outcrops were unfamiliar. Large gulls flew over-

head, but no other dragons could be seen, nor any of their roosts or the dragon tribe's homes.

"Where am I?" he finally asked and turned away from the water to see his little sister, Charlotte, standing feet from him. She wore brown riding leathers, and her long hair was tied in a single braid down her back. She held her hands to her chest, a worried look on her young face. Zander had a fleeting moment to realized she appeared much older than her seventeen years. In fact, the look she gave him with her deep blue eyes had him worried.

"I need to tell you something," Charlotte stated, and Zander saw with concern that tears were trailing down her face. Her skin was so pale in the day's light that faint freckles stood out along the ridge of her cheeks.

"Tell me what, little runt?" he asked, hoping his silly term of endearment might stop the tears and bring a smile to her pretty face.

"I go after our parents," she replied. She turned to look out to sea, crossing her arms over her chest. "Our sister will soon journey beyond the horizon, but you"—she turned to look at him once more— "you will be in the most danger. Earth holds many things Mother didn't know about or failed to tell us about."

"Earth?" Zander asked and finally understood he wasn't dreaming; he was in one of Charlotte's visions. His sister had used her gift of magic and spanned across the universe to bring him to her so she could talk to him.

He knew she had done this before, when their mother was trapped in Midzark as a slave to the old Grand who wished to learn the art of magic from her. Charlotte had been young then, maybe six or seven, but even that young, her magical powers had allowed her to bring their mother across time and space. The vision Charlotte had given to their mother that time had given Tresstéanna hope, and Zander wondered if this would be the same for him.

"You know where I am?" he said as hope sprung into him. Thoughts of being rescued flashed in his mind. If she knew he and his group had been sent to Earth, then maybe someone could come and get them, much like Wizard Leian had retrieved his own mother many years ago.

"I do, but no, no help can come from Genoa for you. Genoa is on a ledge much like you and I are now standing on the edge of this cliff. Much depends on our skills in magic and our love for each other." A single tear fell from her cheek. "I must tell you; you need to find the Fairy Falls to return. But first..." She paused and stepped closer to him as her blue eyes grew wide. "A warning. Never count yourself safe there. There are items that track you on your run. Search for the falls. Belent will know what tool is needed to bring you back, but hurry, while I toil in another place. Our sister's life might be in danger."

"Caylee?" Zander asked as panic bloomed inside him. "What about her?" He moved to step towards her, but Charlotte shook her head quickly and stepped back.

"For now, she is safe, but on her trip across the sea, if her heart betrays her, she will fall." Charlotte continued to shake her head and once again looked out beyond the waters.

Fear ate away inside Zander, and he leaned towards her as she sighed once and squared her shoulders. After taking a deep breath, he saw her give a strong shudder.

"Where do you go? Where are Mom and Dad?" Zander asked, concern for both his sisters now increased.

"I go where I fear the most. I go to hell," she stated and to his horror, her image faded.

Zander bolted straight out of bed. Fear caused sweat to

drip down his face. His mouth was dry, and his heartbeat erratically thumped in his chest.

"And you didn't recognize where you were?" Belent asked Zander once again as the whole group sat around in the largest of the three rooms, after Zander had awoken them.

"I told you, we were on the shore of the ocean, but no," Zander answered. Rey saw him shake his head in frustration. "The cliffs weren't home. I mean, they weren't near the Cliffs of Faro. Maybe further north?"

"She must be going to seek Wizard Leian," Belent said with confidence and a nod of his head.

"Maybe," Zander said with doubt. "I worry more right now about where she said she was heading."

"Hell," Rey said with a shake of her own head. "I have never heard of any place in Genoa called this."

"It isn't in Genoa," Zander said and once again stood to pace the small room. "She said she goes where she feared the most."

"It's a state of mind more than a place, you mean," Belent said with a nod.

"Yes," Zander replied as he continued to move about. Rey knew him well enough to know he felt trapped inside the room when, in reality, they were trapped on Earth.

"We must return as soon as possible," Belent said as he scratched his thin face. The night's growth of hair on his chin was mostly gray, but his brown eyes were sharp enough. "The Fairy Falls," he said, deep in thought and ignoring the others in the room.

"What we really need is a library," Rey repeated her words from the night before.

"Yes, but not all of us can go," Seth said from his perch on the side of the bed. "At least, not all at once."

"We have several missions to accomplish today," Belent said suddenly, turning to study the group.

Zander, Seth, and Rey were assigned the library. Belent and Mika, one of the youngest amongst them at nineteen, were to go shopping for clothing, while Corbin and Avaline were assigned the task of finding different accommodations for the coming night.

"We need something more private and less..." Belent stared around the room. "Crowded."

"And maybe a kitchen," Seth said quickly. "I think food is also in order."

"Always thinking with your stomach," Corbin teased but nodded.

"We will find some food," Corbin said as he counted out the remaining cash. He handed two bills to Zander and two went to Belent.

"Don't forget to get the right sizes," Seth warned as he handed Mika the list of clothing they would need.

"Stop nagging," Mika said. Her gray eyes rolled at Seth as she took the list. She had her mohawk combed down along one side of her dark head and swept around her shoulder to cover her own bright orange tattoo of her dragon.

"I saw the store yesterday; it spoke of a huge sale," Sash said from the corner of the room.

"Don't worry, big guy, we'll get you something to make

you less... large," Mika said with a smile as she held her arms up to indicate his size.

"Why can I not go?" Kenzo whined, and all eyes turned to him.

"Out of all of us, you stand out the most," Rey replied. "We need to find you a hat and a very large coat to cover those big arms of yours," she said with a smile.

"Maybe a poncho," Zander replied with a laugh.

"You are just jealous," Kenzo stated with a frown. He turned to flex his right bicep, which rippled with the movement.

"Ok, you must focus on us the whole time we're all gone," Belent instructed Zander, who stood trying not to roll his eyes at his mentor.

"I know. But just the eight of us today," Belent said and made the others stand next to him and Rey. "Nothing fancy and keep Seth as he is. I think those clothes are closer to Earth's than anyone else's."

Indeed, Seth had dark brown travel trousers on and had only his bottom shirt on. He'd left off his vest and weapons harness, so he now could pass on the streets of Denver without causing too much attention.

Zander scrunched up his face once and the magical image appeared over the group with tasks.

Rey looked down and saw herself wearing not the skimpy dress from yesterday, but a nice pantsuit the color of poppies. She also wore sensible flat shoes of the same color. She smiled up at Zander, who gave her a smirk in return.

"I like the other one better," he told her, and she narrowed her eyes at him and frowned, then finally gave in and stuck her tongue out at him as he laughed.

"Fine, fine. Okay, three hours should do it." Belent looked at the odd little clock. "That means around eleven."

"What if we're delayed?" Zander asked.

"If anyone is delayed, the others will wait another hour, then Kylo and Mateo will go to that person's assignment location. If they too do not come back, the rest must move on. But we will meet back at the entrance point tonight at dark if there are any issues." Belent meant the street where they had first entered Earth and all of them nodded as they understood.

Zander, Seth, and Rey stopped at the front desk on their way out of the hotel. Seth had seen a board with flyers and maps in the lobby yesterday. After getting directions from another desk clerk, thankfully not Missy, they left the safety of the hotel. The sun was bright overhead. Several tall buildings blocked out most of the sky, but it's bright blue was almost blinding.

Dry heat hit them as they exited the building, but a faint breeze blew across Rey face. It carried the stench of the city. The cooler air kept her from growing too hot. More people crowded the street today than the prior night and the street was full of loud cars and billowing smoke.

"Two blocks left and four down," Seth reminded them as they walked.

Rey tried to keep her eyes from going wide in shock. Their vision of the city last night hadn't shown them anything of its true size. The dark city with flashing lights and noises was nothing compared to what lay before them in broad daylight.

She had wondered about Earth's night sky. Since last night, she'd seen no moons in the sliver of sky she'd glimpsed for a brief moment.

Her mind and senses had a hard time taking in every-thing. People rushed everywhere on stone walkways; some were dressed in bright clothes while others wore dirty soil-colored garments. Some, mostly women, had carts or bags over their arms. They had bright colored lips and hair of every color. She noticed a woman with bright purple hair and almost tripped over a loose brick when she turned to get a better look.

Next, there was a large mechanical rectangle lumbering along larger stoneways, some with signs on their sides that advertised for lawyers or stores. Dark smoke bellowed from the machines' rears. Zander told her they were busses.

Carts with food, which smelled wonderful to her, rolled along, and people lined up to order. Two young boys zipped by on flat boards with small wheels stuck on the bottoms. One gave her a whistle and smiled at her as they passed close by. Again, she twisted around for a better look until Zander tugged on her arm.

As they moved, she noticed that the streets were larger and longer than any she had ever imagined. The wide roads almost seemed to disappear into fine pinpoints out in any direction. And everywhere she looked, there were humans.

Men and women were walking, standing, or sitting everywhere. Most were wearing odd dark glasses that covered their faces. Several talked into little squares or were looking at the same items as if transfixed or mesmerized.

"What are those?" she whispered to Zander, who was also looking everywhere at once.

He shook his head and turned back to Seth. "I don't know, but let's keep moving."

The six blocks ended up being almost a full mile of walking. The day turned hotter as they marched along the roads, and the small breeze died away, leaving the air dry and unbearable.

Rey was just starting to think about a cold drink when the library finally appeared before them. It was the weirdest building Rey had ever seen. It was several stories tall and looked like it had been built by a child who couldn't make up its mind.

Red brick mixed with white, and squares mixed with round circles. It had an odd black top floor that reminded her of an upside-down crown. Jagged edges pierced downward from the flat top. Long windows covered the front and other windows shone in the day's light.

"Remember the plan," Seth warned as they approached the front doors.

The massive arch walkways along the front of the building were impressive, but the inside almost took her breath away. A small wooden desk sat to one side of the large room, which was several floors tall. Wood and tile lined the long room and gave the building a grand feeling. Several pictures of the surrounding city lined the walls, which gave her the impression she was still outside.

There were massive walkways leading out of the vast room, each with a sign telling of what could be found beyond. Children's library, Admin, and Plaza were only a few signs she noticed.

As they moved into the room, there was a massive flag hanging over their heads with red and white stripes and a huge square of blue and white stars. She thought of the flag of Genoa, its green background with golden orb of the goddess being held in two white hands that formed a heart. The flag represented the saving of the goddess by their queen. The flag flew above Castle Pines along with the other keeps the queen called home.

"Here. Over here," Seth said, interrupting Rey's thoughts. He steered them down the room towards a door that said maps. "Let's find the falls first."

The building was a mass of mazes. Every room they

passed had two or three more leading out from them, each filled with wooden shelves of books. In one they noticed no books. Instead, there were rows upon rows of desks with the odd square machines the lady at the hotel desk had used.

"It said computer lab," Zander whispered.

"What's a computer?" she asked. He shrugged his broad shoulders.

"Keep going," Seth hissed, and they all left the lab and headed into another section titled fantasy.

"Here," Zander said urgently. He grabbed her arm then led them down one of the aisles. "Mother always said Earth kept everything under fantasy, not history."

"But the falls," Seth warned and pointed towards the door labeled maps.

"Fine, you go find the maps. Rey and I will start looking here," Zander stated with a charming smile.

With a nod, Seth turned and left them to hunt down the location of the Fairy Falls that Charlotte had told Zander about in her vision.

"Where do we start?" she asked as the long rows of fantasy books almost overwhelmed her.

Zander gave the shelves a frustrated look and once again shrugged his shoulders. "We need something about portals."

"Or magic waterfalls." Her eyes scanned the titles nearest them.

"Magic," came an unfamiliar yet sweet voice from behind them.

They both turned and noticed a young boy of about ten standing behind them. His dark face stared up at them, and he flashed a wide smile with white teeth. His black hair was cut short, and he had rather large ears that stuck out. He was missing a tooth near the front and wore thick black glasses that slid slowly down his little nose. Dark blue jeans were topped with a shirt that said, "Han shot first" and had a picture of a dark figure that wore a mask facing off with a man holding a weapon.

"Did you say magic portals?" the kid asked as he blinked behind the wide lenses of his glasses.

"Um," Zander said, his eyes wide with worry. Rey watched him quickly scan the surrounding area as the kid continued to smile up at them.

"Yes, we were hoping to find something fun to read," Rey quickly added, wishing the kid would leave them alone but charmed by his innocent face.

"Well, these are all high fantasy here. There are some kid fantasy books that are great, but I love the originals, you know *Lord of the Rings, The Hobbit* and others." The smile flashed again as dark brown eyes rolled and then landed on a shelf with rather large books set on their right. "See, here's the whole collection. Of course, most have only seen the movies, but I've read each of the books. All of them at least five or six times."

"Um," Zander said again as his eyes fell on one of the leather-bound books.

Rey watched him go pale suddenly and stumble towards her. Reaching out, she quickly grabbed his arm to help him balance. When she looked up into his eyes, he blinked a few times, his green eyes filled with pain.

"Are you ok?" she whispered, fear filling her that he might be getting sick.

"Just a headache." He gave her a weak smile and nodded, she took a quick breath and tilted her head, indicating she didn't believe him. She studied him a second more and when his smile turned sincere, and his green eyes cleared of pain, she nodded once and turned back to the little boy.

"Thank you," Rey said sweetly, then she returned her eyes to Zander's. His color was returning and, after squeezing his hand, she moved to study the books the boy had indicated. "Zander, they are old books," she said under her breath.

"Yeah, about fifty years old now. I think that's when the library replaced the originals," the boy said. He was now standing only a foot away from them. His arms were already filled with several books, but he studied the shelves with yearning. It didn't appear they would be rid of him quickly. "Of course, if you're looking for some out-of-this-world reads, you can always head over to the sci-fi section."

"Out of this world?" Zander quickly said, confusion written all over his handsome face.

"Yeah, over there. You got your *Star Wars*, *Star Trek* and so on. Me, I like a good battle with lightsabers and ray guns, but I always come back to fairy tales." The smile the kid gave them was innocent and quite charming.

Rey felt a little tug of her heart go out to this boy and returned his smile as Zander glanced at the books beside them. Seeing the overwhelmed expression on his face, she turned to study the kid once more and had a brilliant idea.

"Say, do you know any stories that talk of a waterfall taking you to another place?" She bent down so her face was level with his.

The boy scrunched up his face in concentration and thought for a minute. After one big sigh he shook his head. "Only one story I know of. It was written by a hermit or something. It's a new book though. Tells of a band of warriors getting stuck and they have to find their way home. I think it's more of a love story though cause my mother read it, and she loves romantic stories like that." He wrinkled his nose at them.

"Warriors getting stuck?" Rey asked. She felt her face flush and her heart skip several beats. "Where?" she quickly asked.

"Oh, it's over in the new section I think." The boy shifted his pile of books in his hands.

"No, I mean where were they stuck?" she asked, holding her breath without realizing it.

"Oh, that's what's silly. They got stuck here on Earth. I mean, if you're going to write a good story, you got to set it in some cool place far off or out of this world, not here in Denver," the boy said, a pout on his face.

Now there was a buzzing in Rey's ears as she turned her eyes towards the tower of books the boy had pointed at. The books were arranged in a pile on three tables, with the covers of the books facing outward. It was the center table that caught her eye.

She left the boy with a quick thank-you and dragged Zander across the room. The book's cover was dark blue with a bright slash of white that ripped down the middle. When she drew closer, she saw it was a picture of a massive waterfall with the words "Fairy Falls" in bright red letters over the image.

The author's name was at the bottom of the picture, a man named Ben Boon. Slowly she lifted the thick book and turned it around.

She sucked in her breath when she noticed the picture on the back. There, on the back flap, was a picture of Belent the sorcerer.

5

THE QUESTION OR NOT

Zander used his fake Bond information to gain a library card, which allowed them to check out the book that held the likeness of Belent on the back cover.

Meanwhile, Rey kept hissing in his ear questions and concerns that he too had. The discovery of Belent's image alone was enough to raise alarms in his head. Yet, hearing the book's description brought on even more.

"A group trapped on Earth trying to escape to their homeland. Fairy Falls is a MUST read."

"How? Who and even what?" were all whispered harshly in his ear as they searched the library for Seth with their copy inside a bag with the library logo on its cover.

"I don't know," he finally said, stopping dead center of the main hall of the building. "I only know we have to find Seth and get back to the rooms."

"There," Rey said after quickly scanning around. She pointed towards the computer room. "He's sitting at one of those machines."

Zander was shocked to see the dragon warrior bent over the odd box, but he nodded and quickly walked into the room. His shock increased when he saw several pictures of Belent flash on the screen. He read the caption of one picture where Belent was standing with a handsome dark-haired woman. Jewels adorned her neck, and she wore a skinny gold dress that flared out at the bottom. "Ben Boon, famous author and entrepreneur, with his longtime girlfriend Shelly Stratton, at the Gala."

"What?" he started to ask, but Seth quickly waved them over and placed a finger to his lips, indicating they should be quiet.

"Shh. Not here," Seth advised. He bent back over the device.

Seth tapped several buttons on the front of the box and the image changed. This time a dark, blurry video appeared on the screen. It was the image of Zander and his friends magically appearing in the street the night before. There was no sound coming from the image, but writing below stated, "Magical warriors."

"This is worse than I thought," Seth said, quickly turning to look around the room.

Zander and Rey did the same and noticed there were three other people in the room with them. Each had their heads bent over their own device, totally transfixed on their own screens.

"Quickly, adjust our images, face only," Seth whispered urgently at Zander.

"I don't know if I can."

"Yes, you can. Remember when we played a trick on your dad and turned his hair green?" Seth turned to study him, a serious expression on his face. "Do it or we will be in trouble."

Taking a deep breath, Zander called up his birth magic and focused. He concentrated on Rey first. He gave her a longer chin and changed the shape of her eyes to appear squarer, almost like Kenzo's squinted eyes.

Then he turned and studied Seth. Here he gave him facial hair in the form of a goatee. He lengthened his friend's hair and popped some glasses on his face.

After nodding his approval, he turned his focus on himself. He too soon sported facial hair in the form of a bushy beard. Then he shortened his own hair, much like the buzz cut the dragon wizard Col now sported.

"Good, now let's get back to the rooms quickly." Seth hit a single button on the box and the screen of the machine went blank. "Let us hope we are not too late."

As they exited the library, they scanned their surroundings, looking for danger. Zander carried the small bag with the book hidden inside and placed a protective hand on Rey's shoulder. He felt the tension in her arms and knew she too felt scared.

"Seth, what was all that?" she finally asked when they were only a block away from the library.

"They have something called a camera here on Earth. It takes pictures, moving pictures. Someone captured our appearance and show last night and put it on the web." Seth's words confused Zander, but he remained quiet while Seth continued to explain. "It is a place where people can get at the pictures. The library's assistant showed me how to use the box and search for things. I was searching for magic when the image of our arrival showed up. I then found someone who thought that a well-known author of Earth by the name of—"

"Ben Boon!" Zander's interruption had Seth stopping and spinning to look at him with concern on his face.

"Yes, how did you know?" he asked.

"We found his book. Seth, it's Belent!" Rey answered. She tried to grab the bag from Zander's hands.

"Not here," Seth hissed quietly. "And yes, I think it is Belent." Seth nodded and continued walking back to the hotel, ignoring their shock. "Anyway, someone said Belent looked like this man, this author fellow, and I was currently reading what the web was saying about the video when you two found me."

"Charlotte said they had a way of tracking us here," Zander explained, and his hand tightened on Rey's arm.

"I fear there is more to worry about too." Seth then murmured a name that had Zander going cold with fear.

"General Wilberg," Zander repeated, and hatred for a man he had never met filled him. "He can't still be alive."

"I doubt it," Seth replied. "However, there are always those who would step into another's shoes."

"You fear this world's army?" Rey finally asked as she walked quickly beside him.

"My mother told me much, and yes, I fear it. I would be a fool not to be cautious," Zander replied.

They quickly returned to the hotel. Zander kept their new disguises in place, and they quietly bypassed the front desk and headed straight to their rooms.

"I hope everyone is back already," Seth said as they entered the stairway that would take them up the ten flights to their floor.

None of the warriors from Genoa had ever seen an elevator, so they had all been using the stairs. When they rounded the corner on the second floor, the door opened, and Sash stood there waving them out of the stairwell.

"Quickly, here." He urged them forward, his dark face filled with worry.

"What?" Seth started but grew quiet when Sash put a finger to his mouth.

They followed the big man down a long hallway and out another door. This led to an outside stairway, and they quickly descended the steps into a narrow alley.

"This way. Quickly." Sash said no more but turned quickly down the slender walkway between two buildings.

"Should I—?" Zander was going to ask if he should change their appearance again when Sash again made the motion for quiet and continued on.

They walked down the alley and into another one, then two more, each filled with large garbage containers and broken wooden crates. At one point they passed a person lying on a foul blanket, but since the man didn't move, they quickly ran past him.

The sun was growing brighter by the time they finally reached another building. Seth raced up the outside staircase and knocked on the wooden door on level four.

When Kylo answered, they hastened inside and shut the door behind them. Zander saw they were in another hallway, this one similar to the hotel they had spent the previous night in, but the carpet wasn't as clean and there was an odd smell of onions floating in the air.

"This way," Kylo said. He ushered them down a long dark hallway to the first door on the left. "We are still waiting for Belent to get back."

"Back?" Zander asked as he walked into a small hotel room. This room held two beds. One sagged in its center under an ugly orange spread. Kenzo sat on the edge of the other. Mika and Leon were each sitting, propped up against a brown headboard while sharpening their weapons.

"Corbin and Avaline directed us to this hotel but went

out again for food," Mateo explained as he closed the door behind them.

"They still had your illusion on," Mika said as she stood to greet them. "But yours looks different now."

"We are all going to need disguises," Seth said as he held up a hand to the others. "I will tell you when everyone is back. First, why did you move locations before we could get back?"

All eyes went to Kenzo, who blushed boldly across his dark face. His eyes looked downwards and shuffled his feet.

"Well, it appears that a maid comes to clean the rooms each day." The large warrior shrugged his shoulders. "I had no idea."

"Let's just say that, after Kenzo tried out the showers, he forgot his modesty and scared the pretty little maid who was already changing the sheets. We were afraid the forcers would be called," Mika said with a laugh.

"So, nothing bad happened?" Seth asked suspiciously.

"Bad? Ask the maid if it was bad." Mika smirked, and her gray eyes narrowed at the question.

"We'll tell you everything once Belent is back. Where did you say he went?" Zander asked.

"Well, we finished our shopping early, then on the way back to the rooms, the lady at the front desk stopped us and gave him a note." Mika shook her head before anyone could interrupt her. "No, I don't know who it was from or what it said. He came up to the rooms with me and, after hearing about Kenzo's exposure, they helped us move to the new rooms, saying we couldn't wait for everyone to return. Then he took off."

"He's the one who led us here too. Corbin and Avaline had a different hotel picked out, but he insisted we stay here," Kenzo explained. "It was like he knew the way here."

"Did he say when he would be back?" Seth asked. He peeked out the spy hole as he locked the door.

Kylo nodded once, his expression grim. "He said he should be back before dark."

In the end, Seth and Zander told the others what they had discovered while in the library long before Belent returned.

As they talked, the book was passed around for all to see. Zander had lifted his magic, and Rey was once again in her warrior leathers.

Breathing a sigh of relief, she stretched her shoulders once or twice and was shocked to realize how tense she had been while out. She sat next to Mika on the bed and when she was handed the book, she turned to read the back cover as the others continued to talk and speculate about the author and sorcerer.

Adventure waits for a small band from Storlock who find themselves banished to Earth. An evil sorceress casts a spell, and the fairy princess Reanna along with her dashing protector Count Zack soon find that escaping Earth isn't as easy as they hoped.

Fairy Falls keeps them trapped in the non-magical world where electronics and modern-day inventions keep the two on the run from the evil Major Berk. Yet love blooms as dangers threaten to rip them apart.

Come, escape to Fairy Falls and join the adventure of a lifetime with our two heroes. Their story will trap you, much like they were trapped on Earth.

Noting the similarities in the story and her and Zander's names, she quickly dismissed the romantic implications, and turned to read the bio of the author. After a few words, her brows raised as new questions formed in her mind.

Ben Boon the third is heir to the Twisted Pines Inn nestled at the base of the real-life Fairy Falls outside Fernie BC. Bachelor and tycoon, Mr. Boon spends his time writing fantasy stories while maintaining his family's vast estate in the Canadian Mountains.

Mr. Boon has written four best-selling fantasies that captured the hearts of readers of all ages. He finds his inspiration in the beautiful surroundings of the vast forests and mountain ranges of his home in Canada and invites you to "escape" with him into another world.

"Where is Canada?" she asked Seth, who was sitting on the floor under the room's small window.

"I got distracted by the video," Seth informed her with a shrug of his shoulders. "I never found the maps."

Rey nodded then studied the picture on the back of the book. Why did the bio read like this Mr. Boon knew they needed to "escape" from Earth?

"This story sounds similar to ours," she said. She looked up as Zander approached her.

She handed the book to him. A crease formed between his brows as he read. He paused once and reread a sentence before he dropped the book into her lap.

"Sounds like a romance book to me." He shook his head. "But the similarities are there."

"Ah, food," Kenzo said as Corbin and Avaline walked into the room. Corbin had two large bags, and Avaline was carrying odd-looking tubes.

"I've got two more bags of clothes in the other room, if you want to change," Corbin stated as he pointed his chin at

Rey. "You and Avaline and Mika are taking the second room," he explained.

"Only two rooms?" Zander asked as he reached over and grabbed a large sandwich from his friend. "Oh, meat," he exclaimed and, without his twin, who was an avid vegetarian, near to scold him, immediately took a huge bite of the sandwich.

The sandwiches were wrapped in long cylinders that had bright yellow and green writing on them. She was handed a small bag and an odd cup with a round tube sticking out of its top.

"It's a straw. I got you Diet Coke. I don't know what's in it, but I liked it," Avaline said with a smile.

After taking a sip, Rey agreed that it was good and then discovered the bag had crisps in it. They were a little salty for her taste, but the sandwich was amazing.

After she finished eating, she followed Avaline into the second room and changed into a pair of soft blue pants and a buttoned red shirt that her friend had found.

"We got three more shirts and a second pair of pants for you. The boots they had didn't look as sturdy as ours, and I figure the pants will cover them, so I didn't get any shoes for us," Avaline advised her. Her cheeks pinked a little as she held out a gray coat. "This didn't fit me. I wish it did, but I figured you could wear it."

Rey took the jacket, and it fit her very well. She ran a hand over the odd material and smiled. It was similar to her riding leathers, but there was a print inside the deep gray material. It reminded her of her dragon's scales, but a lot smaller.

"Wow. Nice." She studied her reflection in the long mirror on the back of one of the doors in their room.

"Let's see if Belent is back," Mika suggested. The

younger woman was also wearing new clothing, tan pants and an odd pink shirt with a thick jacket that had a white hood attached to it.

Belent hadn't returned, but Rey smiled at the clothing Corbin had chosen for Zander. Black jeans hugged his long muscular legs. Rey took a moment and admired the fit. She also liked the soft green shirt he wore, which matched his eyes, and a light gray sweatshirt.

"I started to read this book," he told her as she neared where he sat on the floor, leaning against the wall. "I think this Mr. Boon knows a lot about Genoa."

Sitting next to him, she glanced at the opened book on his lap. "He writes about Genoa?"

"Well, not Genoa exactly. He calls it Storlock." Zander shook his head. "The main characters are the spitting image of you and me, though."

"He put us in the book?" She plucked it up from his lap. She had seen the similarities in the names and had guessed as much but was still shocked to think her life was in a book here on Earth.

"Read page three," Zander said with a smile. "He has you pegged."

She read and her eyes narrowed when her physical form was described in detail, right down to her long black hair. She read the description of Zack, who had Zander's green eyes and wicked smile, along with his inability to focus on using his magic and some of his immaturity.

"He describes this Zack as a handsome fellow." She tilted her head as she studied Zander. "I don't think there's too much similarity there," she teased, and he elbowed her in her ribs.

"He's back." Seth's words interrupted their teasing, and they jumped to their feet as Seth opened the door quickly.

Seth had taken to standing at the door and looking through the peephole, both to keep an eye out for Belent and to guard the hallway.

When Belent walked into the room, his face was pale, and he was frowning. As the door was shut behind him, he held his hands up to stop the bombardment of questions the warriors were throwing at him.

"Hold on, hold on." He turned to lock the door. "I will tell you all, but first, where is my food?"

The sorcerer sat on the dented bed and ate the sandwich and crisps while he tried to explain all that had transpired since his quick departure.

"First, the note I received had been mailed to the hotel. It is a form of delivery here. When I saw the writing, I was shocked to see my own pen. It said that I needed to move my people right away and gave me directions to this hotel. The note also said we would be safe here for two nights, but we must move again before the third. And yes, there are directions for the next place we should go." Belent took another bite of his sandwich. "Before I go further, the note was indeed from myself."

"But how?" Zander quickly asked as Belent held up his hand again for quiet.

"What I cannot tell you is vast, but this I do know. At some point in my future, I am thrown backwards in time while here on Earth. This 'other' Belent, or Ben as he now calls himself, has been here for over sixty Earth years."

"He lives in Canada," Rey stated as Belent turned to her, his eyes wide with shock. "We have your book here, or his book." She held it out for the sorcerer's inspection.

As Belent read the back cover, he smiled and nodded. "Yes, he told me some of this."

"You talked to him?" Seth asked.

"Yes, over a video phone," Belent explained. "It is a device one of his private men had. The note asked me to go into an office building and meet with a man. I was led into a private room where a machine showed me, well, myself."

Rey thought of the machines at the library and nodded as the sorcerer continued to explain about his visit with himself.

"He reassured me he was me and gave me, in great detail, the story of my life," Belent continued, his face sober. He stared off into the corner of the room, deep in thought for a minute, then he continued.

"He also warned me about Earth and some of the dangers we must avoid." Here Belent set his meal aside and stood to face the group of hardened warriors from Genoa. "Friends, I fear we are already being hunted. From now on, great care must be taken in everything we do."

6

THE HUNT IS HUNTED

Zander and the warriors from Genoa spent that night at the second hotel. Plans were discussed most of the night on how they would all travel north to the falls and meet up with Ben. Before long, they had gotten used to calling the other Belent by this alternative name.

These plans took some thought, as Ben had told them that using public transportation might result in their capture. This left them very few options and a lot of unanswered questions.

"We know we need to join Ben up north; did he say how we are going to get there?" Seth asked impatiently.

Belent shook his head no. He explained that other than their stay at this hotel, Ben couldn't give them too much information. "If we change anything, anything at all, then his previously patterned events also change from what we are currently living," Belent informed them with a shake of his head. "By contacting me, Ben has already altered events. It is this time, let us call it adjusted time, that he knows nothing about."

"Wait, you mean we have already changed what Ben

lived through? But then how is Ben still here? Won't everything we do change his outcome too?" Zander asked and felt a headache forming behind his left eye.

"Magic rules even on Earth, even though it is not practiced here," Belent replied with a shake of his head at his pupil. "Remember, time is much like a river. It flows in many directions."

"Ugh, enough with magic, what about getting back home?" Rey asked, her words laced with frustration.

"The princess mentioned that I would know what tools are needed to bring us back home," Belent stated. He studied Zander, questions filling his dark eyes.

"Yes. She also said we must hurry," Zander replied, thinking back to his dream.

"Ben never mentioned an item, but I think I know what type of item is needed. I just do not know if there is one here on Earth," Belent said with concern.

"What?" Rey quickly sat forward, but Belent held up one of his hands.

"Not here," he said with a shake of his head. "I need to do some research first."

"Is this hotel safe?" Seth asked. All eyes turned to study Belent.

"Ben said the prior place was not safe anymore. He never mentioned anything validating our safety after that. So, no. I think we need to move on from here, with caution. He said the payment card his man gave me would work for a few days. He also mentioned we needed to get cash before the fourth day." Belent showed the odd card the future Belent had provided.

That night, Rey started to read Fairy Falls while Zander and Corbin watched several movies on the TV. Since the other warriors also wanted to watch, and the TV made so much noise, she moved her reading into the second room. However, Avaline and Mika were already there watching a movie of their own. This movie was quieter, but soon Rey found herself distracted by the images and story on the screen and eventually stopped trying to read to watch the story being played out on the screen.

The next day they moved their band to the next hotel. This one was along a major road further out of the city than they had traveled so far. They decided to split up into four groups for their walk to the hotel and had agreed to keep to the side streets.

Zander used his magic to disguise them all during their trek. He had added facial hair for the men, and for the women he adjusted minor details like height and hair color. Rey didn't mind the bright red hair he gave her, but she didn't like the illusion of the very short cut.

"Stop fiddling with it," he scolded her as they walked down the wide streets of Denver. This street had small trees lining one side, and a muddy creek ran along the road's right side. Several people milled about in the faded grass, some lying on dark blankets, others sitting on stone benches along the walkway.

"It feels weird," Rey whined, tugging on one very short red lock.

"It's an illusion." He grabbed her hand away from her hair and held on to it. "Just pretend you're wearing it up." He glanced at her sideways and saw her wrinkle her nose. "What? I like it when you wear your hair up."

"If you two are finished," Seth said from behind them. "We need to turn here."

Zander felt Rey's arm stiffen before he realized what was wrong. They had just turned down the new road when red and blue lights two blocks ahead of them caught his attention. Military and police cars blocked the road and surrounded the hotel. The very hotel where Zander and his friends had been planning to stay.

"Is that our hotel?" Rey asked as they all stopped on the sidewalk, shocked, and dazed by the spectacle of so many lights.

"Quickly," Seth said, pulling on Zander's sleeve. They dashed across the street and down the nearest alley. "Cats, they have the first group already!"

Zander's shock turned to confusion at Seth's words. Then he quicky realized what he had seen beyond the flashing lights, and panic set in.

He had seen Corbin and Avaline being led away from the hotel with their hands behind their backs as several uniformed men had been tackling Sash to the ground. The large warrior had been standing his ground, but Zander was sure that with that many enemies, even Sash would surely lose the battle.

"Stay here," Seth whispered, and he quietly walked to the edge of the building and peeked around quickly. "Here comes the other group." Soon, Belent, Kenzo, and Kylo raced into the dark alley.

"Where are the others?" Belent asked as he bent over to catch his breath.

"Corbin, Sash, and Avaline are up there beyond the lights," Seth said, his face dark with worry. "Mateo, Mika, and Leon were behind you."

"Here we are," Mika said as she raced up and embraced Rey. "Were we discovered?"

"We must have been," Zander said. He crept to the edge of the building to peek out at the flashing lights again. "Look, there's the hotel manager from last night."

"Get back." Seth tugged on Zander's arm.

"No, I'm using magic, I'm invisible," Zander said as he pushed his arm away from his friend. Sure enough, the lower half of his body was visible, but from mid-shoulder to the top of his head, he was invisible.

"Hold on. They have Sash on the ground now. That's either going to hurt or anger him," Zander said as a man stomped on Sash's ribs. Sure enough, the large warrior grabbed the man's foot and flung him two yards before he was once again tackled by six new men, all in black.

"What is happening?" Rey demanded next to him.

"They put Corbin and Avaline in a black van, but Sash is making quite a muck of it all. Hang on, I'm going to get a closer look."

"No, you won't," Rey warned next to him, grabbing his arm. "At least, not without me."

He looked down at her, then nodded. "Hold my hand."

Hand in hand, Zander walked Rey up the street. He felt Belent's presence next to him, the sorcerer's magic keeping him as invisible as they were. As they neared the end of the block, the sounds of the struggle reached their ears.

"Right here. You check out the van, and I will get close to Sash," Belent whispered.

"Right," Zander said. He squeezed Rey's hand. "We are invisible, but they can still hear us, so be quiet," he warned. He felt her return squeeze, which he took to mean she understood.

They had reached the newly placed barricades and spent some time weaving around people and obstructions before they could approach the black van his friends had been thrown into. Two guards stood sentry next to the double-wide doors at the back of the machine. These guards restricted them from getting too close to their friends.

However, even before they reached the van, Zander could hear voices shouting.

"Crazy man, don't know what you're talking about," Corbin shouted. "Hey, get your hands off her." This statement was followed by a deep grunt and a laugh from his friend. "See, my lady can take care of herself."

"You will submit," came a harsh low voice that sent chills down Zander's spine. "Aliens have no rights here."

"Aliens? Man, like from space. Are you crazy?" Corbin hollered as another grunt was heard.

"Please tell your friend to stop resisting. We have proof," the harsh voice said.

"Proof? Man, are you talking about that fun video we put out?" Corbin asked with another chuckle. "Man, that was a, what do you call it, a publicity stunt." Zander sighed a breath of relief as Corbin kept to the cover story that he and Seth had made up in case any of them ran into someone who had seen the video of their first night on Earth.

"Where is she? Where is your leader? The one called Anna?" Zander's breath caught in his throat as Rey tugged on his hand.

Turning, he saw a large man in a dark uniform march up to the van. His silver hair was cut short, and he had a bushy mustache that covered his top lip. Brown eyes squinted as the man frowned at the two guards who stood at attention. The placed their right hands to their forehead in a salute, and Zander could smell the fear emanating from the two guards at the new man's approach.

"Where?" The man barked the question, which came out more like an order.

"General Wilberg, they are in here," one guard quickly replied. At the man's name, Zander felt the air leave his lungs in a large whoosh.

"General Wilberg?" Rey heard Zander hiss as they tried to get even closer to the van.

Rey studied the van and the two large guards. She knew they could easily be dispatched, but the remaining forces that surrounded the van could not.

She tugged on Zander's hand and tried to get a look at the front of the van. If they could gain control of the van, then they could drive off with their friends. They might have to bash through some barriers, but she didn't think that would be a problem.

"Do you know who I am?" the general demanded from inside the van now.

"Jack Nicholson?" Corbin asked snidely. Rey held in her snicker when their friend mentioned a man who had been in one of the movies that they had watched on the TV box in the men's room the night before.

Corbin and Zander had spent as much time as possible watching the odd box, or television, since their arrival. All the men had liked the military movies, but she preferred the news. She found the Denver nightly news gave her knowledge about what Earth was really like, and it frightened her very much.

"I'm the one who hunted the witch, Anna, for years, General Wilberg responded as Rey finally managed to peek in the front of the van. She felt instant disappointment when she saw all the gears and levers, but Zander gave her hand a squeeze and remained near the front of the van, where the driver's door stood open.

"General, what are your orders?" came the harsh voice again.

"Corporal, ensure the big one is chained up and thrown in here. Make sure no one touches them. We will move them to the base." Worry filled Rey, and she felt Zander's hand tense.

She felt his lips near her ear and heard him whisper instructions. She quickly released his hand and climbed into the front of the van, scooting far from the gears and wheel to wait.

Despite her twisting and turning, she still couldn't see any part of her body as she sat waiting. She knew the minute Sash's large body was thrown into the back of the van, as the whole vehicle shook when her friend landed in the cargo area. As the minutes ticked away, worry about Zander's plan started to fill her. But his idea was good. The plan would not fail, she reassured herself.

She caught her breath when an unknown military man climbed into the van and sat behind the wheel. The man had short jet-black hair and gray eyes that matched his uniform. Sweat slid down her back and her mouth went dry until the man turned and winked in her direction.

"Move over, love. I think you're squishing Belent." The man reached down and started the van's engine.

"Are you sure you can drive this thing?" came the disembodied voice of the sorcerer.

"Ye of little faith," Zander, disguised as one of the military men, said with a smile. "I watched that movie with the cool cars just yesterday."

Rey held her breath for a moment. "You're not going to drive like they did, are you?" she demanded, trying to keep the fear from her voice. When Zander chuckled, she knew she had failed in hiding her fear.

"Ah, here we are. Look how nice they are at moving those blockades for us." Zander waved at the two uniformed men as they made room for the van to leave the area.

"Now, shall we go and pick up the rest? This van will do nicely to get us north I think." Again, the cocky little wink was sent in her direction.

"What do we do with the men in the back?" Belent asked as Zander drove down the street.

"Hm. Any ideas?" Zander asked as the van moved a little too close to another parked car.

"Also, how do we get away from the lead car?" Belent asked.

"I'm thinking. There's another car behind us too," Zander said with a shake of his head.

"Can we lose them?" Rey asked. She sucked in a quick breath when Zander yanked on the wheel. The van pulled a sharp left and then quickly sped up. The van went on two side wheels as he took another turn at high speed. "We're invisible now."

"You mean the whole van?" she screamed as he took another corner.

"Yeah, but we've got to get our friends fast, then get out of town," Zander said as his disguise faded. Rey was visible once again, but this time inside an invisible vehicle.

"How long can you keep this up?" Belent asked as he too popped into focus.

"I don't know. The van is huge."

Rey saw a bead of sweat trickle down his temple.

"There," she hollered as they bowled down the same alley their friends still stood in. The dragon warriors raised their weapons at the sound of the van, and then their eyes grew wide, indicating Zander had dropped the invisibility illusion that covered them.

"Quickly, get inside the back," Rey shouted. She heard her people quickly overcome the three guards that had been stationed in the back with her friends.

"We're all in," came a quick shout, and Zander nodded once and started the van again. His face focused as they raced down another alley then two more.

"If we move into the streets, it will be hard to drive while invisible," Belent said with a shake of his head.

"We aren't." Zander grunted.

"Aren't what?" Rey asked with concern as her eyes went wide. "Invisible?" Panic set in as she studied their surroundings, fearful that at any moment they would be surrounded by military men and flashing lights.

"No, we are disguised. It's much easier than invisibility." Zander returned his gaze to the road ahead as he drove.

When they turned onto a main street, she caught the van's reflection in the nearest window. She saw a rather nasty green van with a bent fender and dents all about its sides.

"We're a plumbing van," she said with a laugh. She turned to Belent, who stared at her in confusion. "It says 'Plumber Inc. We give a crap about your pipes.'" She laughed.

7

AUTOMOBILES AND PLANES

Zander snaked in and out of the traffic while trying to pay attention to the road signs. His illusional magic kept the van disguised, but it didn't keep it from hitting anything.

"Am I on the right road?" he asked nervously as another road sign with six street names pointing in several directions passed by too quickly. "What direction are we heading now?"

"Yes, it says north," Rey told him.

Zander kept seeing her glance behind them. He too was worried they were being chased.

"Keep the disguise up if you can. At the next road try and change it, just in case," Belent urged from between them.

"There, a small moving van. You can use that disguise," Rey provided. Zander nodded and gave a faint grunt in agreement.

"Here, turn here, on the major road. It says it heads north." Belent pointed to their right.

Zander swerved to the right after using the mirrors to

make sure he wouldn't hit anyone. He turned towards the main road. They climbed a small hill and came to a dead stop when they hit traffic.

"What is this?" Rey asked. Panic laced her voice as the van jerked when it stopped.

"I think it's just traffic. You know the news was all about rush hour," Belent provided with a huff.

"Do you think they know?" Zander asked as he once again glanced into the mirrors.

"The escape was subtle. It could be hours before they realize anything is wrong," Belent advised with a shake of his head.

"Belent, you said you might know what item is needed. I hope it isn't in this city," Rey stated.

"Me too," Belent replied as Zander inched the van forward a few feet.

"Any idea how long this traffic is?" Rey asked.

After fiddling with the dash, Belent found the radio and turned it on. It took a while longer before he found a station that was covering the traffic.

"Accident on the turnpike," the radio voice said. *"Hope you're not in a hurry today."*

It took them fifty Earth minutes, according to the van's dashboard clock, before they left the shadow of the tall buildings of downtown Denver. The roads were filled with cars winding in and out of one another, which kept them completely focused on their path, and Zander's driving.

It took a rather long hour and a half before they reached the first fields of long dry grasses. After those came homes, which filled their vision for as far as they could see. The only constant during their drive that day were the huge mountains to their left, which amazed them.

"The Rockies," Zander advised them with a smile as he drove on. "Mother spent a lot of time in them."

"There's snow on the tops of them," Rey stated, and Zander smiled at the wonder in her voice.

"Yeah, Mother said that after seeing the Rockies, all the mountains in Genoa seemed tame, except the Cleveites." He quickly looked at the mountains before casting his concentration back to the narrow lines on the bumpy road. He found it hard to keep the van inside the lines, but it appeared all the other drivers did too, as most kept weaving in and out of them, though it seemed their movements were just an attempt to gain a slot ahead of the next car.

"Well, we need to end up on the other side eventually," Belent advised with a shake of his head. "The map I glanced at briefly on the news showed that this mountain range goes all the way up into Canada."

"I think we're going to need food before then," Rey added, and her eyes scanned ahead.

It was several more hours before they felt safe enough to stop. Zander had changed the van's appearance to look like a passenger van. White lettering showed it was a shuttle van. He also hoped this would explain why twelve people popped out when they eventually found a small restaurant off the main highway.

"We're going to need maps and supplies too," Belent urged as he scanned their surroundings.

"I think the machine needs gas too," Zander warned.

As they stood in line to order their food, Corbin said a little too excitedly, "I can drive."

They had split into small groups to enter the restaurant to cause less suspicion. Each person was disguised by Zander's magic.

Zander had decided that the van should carry older

people and had given gray hair and bent shoulders to his robust warrior friends. He gave Seth a cane and smirked at the rather bad hair piece he had given his friend. The nasty brown sweater didn't help either, but it was all part of the illusion.

Belent used the credit card that Ben had provided to pay for all the meals. The girl didn't even look up but proceeded as if she saw vans full of elderly people shuffle around the restaurant daily. When Belent was finished paying, he asked the clerk where he could get cash.

"The gas station has an ATM machine," the young lady said with a smile. She pointed across the street as she finished their order.

Thirty hamburgers, twelve shakes, and various orders of something called 'fries' later, they all piled back in the van. For now, Zander continued to drive but Corbin sat next to him and studied the controls with a deep longing in his eyes.

"We have to figure out how to fuel this thing," Rey said from the other side of Corbin. Like his friend, the leader of the dragon warriors also wanted to learn how to drive, but she had made an excuse for now, saying that more than two of them should know how to control the van.

"Look," Zander said as he slowed the van towards the gas station. "See that woman? Watch how she is doing it while I pull up."

Corbin was the one who figured out the pump that put the fuel in the small circular tube hidden in the van's left side. Belent had to use the card first before the fuel would start, then he quickly disappeared into the station on a quest for maps. The others needed to use the facilities and also disappeared into the store.

After watching Corbin for a minute, Zander followed his friends into the small building.

When he entered, he noticed rows upon rows of food. There were glass doors behind which were cold drinks of numerous sizes, each in bright bottles.

After studying the interior, he decided more food, for later, would be ideal. His excitement increased when he found bags of the crisps they had enjoyed, and he was soon lost in the variety of the selections.

When Rey joined him a few minutes later, Zander had his arms full of bags. He had two containers of bottled water and was contemplating something called 'Snickers.'

"Trouble," Rey said, leaning close, her eyes on something two inches above his left shoulder. Her dark brows were drawn together.

"What?" he asked as she shook her head.

"There is a screen above the counter that shows our true forms," Rey warned, her eyes wide with shock. "Not your illusion."

"What? What do you mean?" he asked, still facing her.

"Remember the video of us when we first arrived? It's like that but"—she raised one hand and touched his shoulder— "it's live, and I can see beyond your illusion of me and you."

"Has anyone noticed?" he asked. He turned to see Belent still pondering maps.

"No, but let's not stick around to find out." She grabbed a handful of the Snickers and then dragged him towards the front.

"Uh, Ben," Rey said as they approached Belent. "We have to go."

"One moment," Belent said, distracted as he studied the

back of a folded map. Belent didn't appear to notice Rey's use of the odd name.

Rey leaned forward and whisper something in the sorcerer's ear. Belent quickly nodded then grabbed three maps from the stand and turned towards the counter, a broad smile on his face.

"Ah, I think this will do it," he said and as Zander and Rey watched. He waved a hand at the monitor, which was set above and behind the clerk. The dark-haired woman in the blue uniform looked bored and tired but gave them a polite smile. When the screen went black, the sorcerer's smile widened, and he asked the clerk calmly. "Can I use your cash machine?"

Zander breathed a sigh of relief when they all piled back in the van. This time Rey sat in the back with the other warriors, while Belent and Corbin remained up front with him as he drove. When they were once again headed back towards the main road, Zander voiced his concerns and questions to Belent.

"Why didn't my magic work on the machines?" he asked.

Belent shook his head as he studied one of the maps from the passenger seat. "It could be you were not concentrating enough. Or maybe your illusional magic does not work on the devices of this world." He sighed. "Either way, we will need to be careful from now on."

They drove several more hours, using the maps to guide

their way north. They hit a third construction zone, and Zander felt his impatience grow when the traffic slowed once again. It appeared the other drivers also felt the impatience because cars were weaving in and out around him. He had several near misses and discovered the van's horn during the second close call.

As the day grew to an end, they finally stopped for dinner just beyond the border of Colorado. A restaurant called the Saloon had beefsteaks the size of the plates they were served on. Loud music pumped out of hidden speakers as they were seated. There was a large stage against one wall where he guessed that musicians could play.

Zander didn't use the same image from lunch. He adjusted each appearance slightly, feeling this would be less noticeable if there were any video cameras around.

They all sat around the large table and ate as if they hadn't eaten in days. Sash and Kenzo ordered second plates, but the others were satisfied with one serving.

Zane nibbled on Rey's remaining side mash, a favorite item served with a dark brown gravy poured over, while Belent focused on the maps.

"I worry the general will track us. We will need to leave false trails," Belent said, his eyes momentarily raised to study a large stuffed animal along one wall. "We don't want to get caught off guard again."

"I don't want to split up," Rey stated as she slapped Zander's hand away from her plate.

"I agree," Zander said as he snuck another bite. "How much further away are these falls?"

"Best guess, about two days." Belent shook his head. "However, I worry the direct path will not be possible."

"Why not?" Rey asked. She finally pushed her plate

over, so it sat directly in front of Zander. He immediately ate the remaining potatoes with a grin and wink.

"If this is the same general who tracked your mother—"

"It is," Zander assured him.

"Well, then the stories the queen told of this foe leave me worried. I fear the trouble we had in the city of Denver is small compared to what this man could cause us, if we are not vigilant." Belent scanned the restaurant, as if he expected General Wilber to walk in and sit down next to them.

"But how is this the same man that tracked Mother? I thought time here was shorter?" Zander asked as he finished the food left on Rey's plate.

Belent shook his head and turned his focus to Zander. "There is much I do not understand. The first is how we got here. The second is how there is another me. And I am afraid the list goes on from there, so much that my head hurts," the sorcerer said truthfully.

"I know how we got here." Rey's statement had Zander and Belent turning to her in stunned silence.

"You know?" Belent finally asked.

She nodded her head and looked at Zander, her eyes full of thoughts. "You know too. At least you should."

"The mist," he finally stated. He felt stupid for not coming to this conclusion earlier. "But what is the mist?"

"Well, that I don't know," Rey exclaimed with a frustrated look on her face. "I never studied magic, but I know defenses against magic are sometimes futile."

"Yet I never felt it until we were thrown to this place," Belent said.

Zander shook his head. "No, it wasn't activated until I stepped into the ring of stones."

The sorcerer's eyes lit up with understanding. "It was a trap for you," Belent said.

"Just like your parents." Rey placed her left hand on top of Zander's. Her brown eyes were full of empathy and concern for him, and he felt something deep down inside him, something close to remorse. He felt something else too, something he wasn't able to pinpoint. Not when he was surrounded by noise and his friends, and danger.

"So, do you think they are here too?" Belent's question interrupted Zander's innermost thoughts. He saw Belent scan the restaurant again.

"No. But I think what happened in Parian was a test." Zander twisted his hand so he could hold Rey's small dark hand, which sat on the table. He smiled when she tried to tug her hand out from his, but she finally gave up and left her hand in his.

"But those people in Parian died," Belent stated, and Zander thought he heard fear in his deep voice.

"A test that failed, but I bet there were other tests that succeeded." He thought back to other reports that had reached the castle. Some had come after the disappearance of the families. "There was a family that disappeared south of the trade station. When was that?"

"Two days after the first disappearance," Seth said as he leaned closer to join their conversation. "And another day after that, the small village near Mirror Lake reported a family of trolls that went missing."

"Two tests," Belent said deep in thought.

"One for your parents, and one for you?" Rey whispered with understanding.

This thought filled him with fear for Caylee. If there had been a trap set inside the castle for his parents, and one for him, then there could be another for his twin.

He thought of his parents, his mother so small yet strong. She was resourceful, but her years on the throne and not in the training yard might not serve her well.

His father still trained, and he was hopeful they were together, wherever they were. Kriston was large and strong. Zander was built like the king, large of shoulder and tall.

Then his thoughts turned to his younger sister. The dream she had sent him still bothered him. Hell. What did Charlotte mean by that word? Their mother had told stories of a hell place when they were younger, using descriptions of a burning underworld ruled by a demon. Charlotte couldn't mean this place, as Zander thought it didn't exist in Genoa. But he was no longer in Genoa himself, so maybe she was traveling to another world much like he had been sent to Earth?

"Where do we go from here? How do we get back?" he finally asked. Fear had his stomach tightening, and the food he had just eaten threatened to return.

"North, for now. I see one main road from this place and hope the general hasn't traced us quite yet. Once we reach a crossing road, we will think of leaving false trails." Belent shook his head. "No plans will be spoken while we are here. However, we might want to exchange our transport machine, maybe get two machines instead?" he speculated. After a moment of silence, he continued, "And I need to find the item that will enable me to cut our way back to Genoa."

"Cut?" Zander asked as he finally released Rey's hand and rubbed his now unsettled stomach.

"The barrier between this world and our own has been sealed. I doubt the Orick would yield even with the right magic," Belent told them with a sad look on his face. "Whatever we do to get back home, it will leave a scar in both places. But first, we must find the tool we need to cut or rip our way home."

"Then what?" Rey asked.

"Then we must find who is behind the mist and stop them."

8

THE HIGH PLAINS

They didn't find a replacement vehicle in the small town where the restaurant was located. Nor the next town. Before dark, however, they came to a large city where the streets were lined with lights and many buildings.

Rey didn't like Denver, and this city felt similar with its vast streets. As a dragon warrior, she had been raised in the warrior way, riding dragons on the high cliffs along the shoreline. She'd been born in a countryside with beautiful forests and had been raised living in tents. That was more her style.

Now she now studied row upon row of streets and odd homes and buildings. Most of the windows were filled with lights, but some were dark and foreboding.

"What are we looking for, again?" Corbin asked as he sat next to her in the front of the van.

"Another van, one that wasn't originally our enemy's," Zander replied as he bent over the steering wheel and studied the streets.

"But why?" Rey asked.

"Belent says this one may be tracked. Even with my

magic changing its appearance." Zander shook his head. Not even he understood the sorcerer's reasoning behind the switch in vehicles.

"Will I get to drive the next machine?" Corbin asked.

"We may end up with two if we can't find one big enough."

Corbin leaned out the window, looking for their replacement vehicle.

In the end, they found a large truck that fit the sorcerer's requirements. It was sitting in an empty parking lot that she guessed was a school. The truck looked like it hadn't been moved for a while, as dust covered the front window, but the back of the vehicle was enclosed and empty.

"Can you start it?" Zander asked Belent as the sorcerer leaned closer to the driver's door. Belent rested one of his hands on the doorknob, and blue light glowed around the lock. He pulled the door open, smiled at them, and nodded. "I believe I can."

"I get to drive," Corbin stated, pushing his way eagerly into the seat.

The front seat only allowed two in its small, cramped space, so Belent sat up front with Corbin to aid him in navigating the streets. Zander needed a break and some sleep, so he and the others climbed into the back and closed the large sliding door behind them. Rey thought it smelled of dust and dirt, but it wasn't an unpleasant smell. She settled on the floor with her friends.

Without any windows, time slowed, and every bump or turn seemed to be exaggerated. Soon her back hurt and she felt slightly nauseous.

"Here, lean against me." Zander tugged her gently over towards him and tucked her under his right arm.

She thought for a minute about how odd it was that

the prince had started showing her his gentle side since they had been here on Earth. Before, in Genoa, they had only had a working relationship, one where she protected him, a job she had often felt he resented. He had never shown up for dragon drills on time, and even during those practices, he was often distracted. She had always felt like he wanted to be somewhere other than running attack drills with her.

Yet now, when they all were in danger, it appeared he had taken on the role of protector. The role suited him much better, and he appeared to be more comfortable with it.

When they were children, Zander and Caylee had been raised within the dragon tribe. Rey remembered the royal family spending many summer days in the tribe's village. She and Caylee were still close friends, despite the princess's lack of interest in learning the warrior's ways.

Rey knew that the nature of Caylee's magic bonded her more strongly with the dragons they rode than with their fighting skills. And Rey respected her for her kind heart, even if her friend couldn't throw a hard punch or do a good battle drill.

Caylee and Zander were so different that it always amazed Rey that the two were twins. Caylee had dark looks, so like their father, and was small of build. Delicate was how Rey would describe her. Zander, on the other hand, had his mother's coloring but his father's build. Rey silently thanked the goddess for this fact.

Zander loved to spar and study the warrior ways, but he grew lazy when it came to constant training. The prince seemed to grow restless easily whenever she or Belent asked him to practice his magic during drills.

Yet it seemed his attitude had changed since they'd

come to Earth. It appeared that he now liked using his magic to protect them all.

It felt nice to rely on him and his magic for protection in this unknown world, though she hated to admit it, even to herself. She could still kick his butt if he fell out of line, but she liked seeing his magical powers.

"I know you are worried about your magic not working against the machines," she whispered finally. She felt him tense a little.

"It appears I have limits even I didn't know about," he replied softly.

She shifted a little to ease her back and turned to look up at him. The truck had a little light above the wide door. Its faint yellow glow didn't do much to illuminate the enclosure, but she was able to see him turn his eyes towards her.

"I know you worry about your family." Again, she felt him tense and then he took a big breath and relaxed again.

"Charlotte is only seventeen," he finally replied.

"If I remember correctly, you were only seventeen when you took on the Barracoota in the northern forest," she said with a smirk.

"That was different," he mumbled.

"And weren't you only fifteen when you took Bree Nu out to the southern island all by yourself?" she teased.

"My mother knew I was going to do that. At least I left her a note."

"The point is, I know Charlotte. She is stronger than you give her credit for," Rey said warmly.

"But she is more of a bookworm than a fighter." Zander's use of one of his mother's odd expressions focused Rey's worry on the missing queen and king.

"Is she really going after your parents? Charlotte, I mean?"

"She said they are in hell. At least I think she said they are there." His brow furrowed as he thought back to the magical communication he'd had with his young sister.

"How about Caylee?" she asked, trying to distract him.

"Captain Adams will take care of her. She also will have Wizard Col to protect her once he arrives at Castle Pines."

"You sent for him?" she asked, feeling relief that the greatest elder of her tribe would be taking care of her friend.

"Caylee did. At least I told her to." Zander absently rubbed a hand up and down Rey's right arm, distracting her from her next question. "She was to send for Leian and Shiarra too. Also, my cousin Calob, king of Matera."

"I haven't met him. Is it true he was once turned into a monster?" She tried not to focus on his touch.

When a chuckle emitted from his chest, she smiled at the sound. Then she returned her gaze to his eyes as he looked down at her.

"A Speculum." He smiled. "Yes, my uncle, the old king, had turned him into a metal creature. But my mother and father saved him from that fate. You have, however, met his twin, Colab. Remember when he and his family came to visit the tribe three years ago?"

"Ah, the ones who traveled all the way from Midzark?" She smiled at the memory. The man had been so like King Kriston that she had instantly been charmed by him and his wife, a pretty dark-haired beauty who spent most of her time talking to their tribe's healer. They had brought their four children with them, two girls and two boys, who had been eager to learn about the dragons. All of them had awe and wonder on their faces.

"You know, Colab was once bonded with a Scarent."

His statement shocked her, and she tried to hide the

shiver that ran through her at hearing the dangerous snakes' name. "Really?" Another shiver ran up her spine.

Another chuckle came from Zander as he quickly ran a finger up her arm. This move caused her to squeal in horror and a full laugh came from Zander this time. "Snakes. I never knew you were scared of anything," he teased, and she gave him a full punch in his stomach for this joke.

"Not all snakes, just those ones." She crossed her arms in defense.

They talked for a while more about his large and odd family. Then she heard some odd noises and looked around the truck for the source, soon determining it was her warrior friends snoring.

After leaning her head against Zander's shoulder, she too dropped off to sleep as the truck lumbered down the road. As she slept, her dreams were filled with odd stories of dangerous travels under the ground, large families and friends, a globe which held their goddess, Genoa, and, yes, snakes.

Zander woke when the truck came to a complete stop. He sat up and felt the pain in his right arm where Rey had pinned it against the side of the truck as she slept.

When Belent opened the back door and peered in, Zander noticed that the sky was still dark, and it smelled slightly of rain. Rey bolted up next to him, and he rubbed the pain out of his arm and smiled down at her.

"Bathroom break, and I need to see you two." Belent pointed at Zander and Rey.

"Is there food?" Kenzo grumbled as he rubbed the sleep from his eyes.

"Always thinking with your stomach," Seth said as he moved past them and immediately walked to the bathroom buildings. They had previously discovered rest stops, which had full facilities, including food machines.

Rey climbed out of the truck behind Zander. Corbin stood behind Belent, a worried look on his face. His red hair was disheveled, as if he had been running his fingers through it.

"I hope you're right," Corbin mumbled, and then he moved off to follow the others to the bathrooms.

"I think I found what we need," Belent stated as he studied them. "I did a finder's spell and made a seeking map. I used something from Genoa to point me in the direction." He shook his head and held the map out.

Zander looked at the Earth map, one that appeared to contain the whole country. It amazed him how large this land was, and he had to remind himself that Genoa was probably large too, when she wasn't divided into pieces.

The goddess Genoa had segregated several evil creatures, all of whom had traveled to her chosen planet hundreds of years ago. This separation kept these monsters from her own children in an attempt to keep them all safe from each other.

As he studied the map, he noticed a small tear north of their current location, west of a town called Sheridan and north of two large mountains.

"Do you know what it is?" Rey asked as she leaned in and studied the map in Zander's hands.

"I do not, but I do know there is a museum there, something they say holds Native treasures." Belent shook his head.

"A museum?" Zander asked and understood why the sorcerer was so grave. "Not some item out in the wild, but something that may be guarded?"

Belent nodded his head again and studied them. After taking a deep breath, he turned to study the building their friends had disappeared into. "We will all be in danger when we try and retrieve the item, whatever it may be," Belent stated, his eyes still on the building.

"You want to split up," Rey stated, shock in her voice.

"I worry," Belent replied.

"I think we should stick together." Rey planted her feet, putting her hands on her hips in a determined stance.

"I think we can compromise," Zander said. He turned as some of the warriors came back out to the truck. "But before we make any decisions, let's get the lay of the museum first. Then we will need a plan."

Zander gave Corbin a break and drove the truck after the stop. Belent sat in front with him, as the distance to the museum wasn't very long.

Belent used his magic to disguise the details of the truck, in case there were any video machines.

The early morning sky showed Zander lots of stars and only one moon, which was small and quartered. Its path kept track with them until it finally disappeared behind a mountain range to their left. Zander guessed it was the same mountain range that he had seen in Denver but couldn't be sure.

"Here, we have to get off this road and move over along this smaller side road for a while," Belent advised him.

Zander took the exit and followed Belent's guidance, heading back north on a different road.

"We have a lot more turns ahead. I just hope we do not go through another big city. Those roads are confusing," Belent admitted.

Zander smiled, then his brows drew together in concentration.

"Belent, if we have to split up, what do you suggest?" he asked as he looked for their next turn.

"I think Rey's partially right. I don't want to send the others ahead, in case they are walking into a trap," he replied.

"You don't think Ben—"

"No, I trust him. Or me," Belent said quickly. "However, I worry that once we are split, we will never join up again."

"And if we have the item, then they won't get back with us to Genoa," Zander provided, speaking his fear out loud. "If we have to steal an item from this museum, how do you suggest we go about it?"

"My boy, you forget we have something this world does not hold." Belent smiled over at him in the dark cab of the truck. "We hold magic."

The sky was just starting to lighten when they drew close to wide fields that surrounded the museum. The orange sun shone its rays on the odd museum building. The light gave them a clear view of a wood and red stone structure halfway hidden on a grassy hilltop. Glass windows and doors led into the building, but beyond that, the inside was a mystery.

"It is quite unique," Belent said, and Zander heard wonder in the sorcerer's voice.

"It's pretty," Zander exclaimed with a nod of his head. "But what dangers will it hold?"

"And what is the item?" Belent nodded and instructed Zander to continue driving around the driveway.

"Look, there's another building." Zander pointed, but Belent shook his head.

"No, what we seek is in the first one." The sorcerer pointed towards the building inside the hill. "I can feel it."

"There's a small forest up ahead. We could leave the truck there and try to get access to the museum," Zander suggested.

"It might be better if we had two vehicles," Belent thought out loud. "Too bad our dragons are not available." A wicked grin spread on his face as he leaned forward to study the small strip of trees ahead of them.

"This is too sparse for any cover." Zander drove down the road, away from their target.

"It is mostly fields," Belent confirmed.

"We don't want the truck too far away." Zander turned the truck back towards the building. When they got back to the parking lot, they were shocked to see two cars already in the parking lot.

The sun was now making the sky a bright blue, and they could see the mountain range behind the museum. No snow covered these smaller peaks, but the range was still quite impressive.

"Let's go back to the little town first and formulate a plan," Belent advised and once again Zander turned the truck back down the road.

"I think I already have an idea," he said with a smile.

Belent paled slightly at his words.

9
____

A SHARP AX

Two hours of talking resulted in a crazy plan, one that Rey still wasn't sure would work.

The plan had to net them the object, an item that Belent needed to first locate, then acquire. It also needed to allow a safe escape afterwards. But the trickiest part was that it required the large group of twelve to split up and then, at a later time, safely rejoin.

"I still don't like splitting up," she complained as she sat next to Zander in the front of the van. Belent was squeezed next to her as Zander drove them back to the museum, which should have opened by now.

"There's a lot at risk here, but Corbin knows what to do if we're caught," Zander said as he maneuvered the truck down the road leading back to the little museum.

"If the past Belent is to be trusted, then why isn't he helping us more?" She heard the Belent next to her take a deep breath.

Rey had been using the driving time to continue reading Fairy Falls. The book had started out explaining about the fictional world of Storlock. She was on chapter four and had just reached the part where the band had been pulled from their world and into Earth.

The similarities were there, yet Ben had written several differences. For example, it was Zander, or rather Zack, who was the protector on their home world, not Rey. There were also fifteen warriors who traveled with them, and one was a land sprite.

With each page Rey read, her worry that their whole story and lives were hidden in the pages increased.

She had quickly flipped ahead when Belent had voiced his thoughts of the item being in a museum. She was concerned their intent to rob the museum of an item was written in Ben's book. She was relieved to see nothing of their thievery anywhere amongst the pages. But even this fact had her worried.

"Again," Belent said as he shuffled his legs to make more room—the front of the truck didn't fit three people comfortably— "he explained that interference would result in a change in his past and our future. It might mean we don't make it back to Genoa at all."

"I know, I just don't like splitting up." She felt ashamed and agitated.

"Ah, here we are, Belent." Zander cast a quick look at the sorcerer, who immediately raised his hand. A faint blue light emitted from Belent's fingers and spread out quickly towards the building.

Rey knew that if there were any security cameras, they were now disabled by magic. Then the sorcerer turned his magic upon himself and disappeared. She could still feel him sitting next to her, so she knew he was still there using his invisibility magic.

"Perfect," Zander stated, and Rey saw the muscles in his face tighten in concentration as he activated his own magic.

Rey, still amazed every time the prince worked his illusion magic, watched in wonder as the front of the truck changed. A sleek black hood replaced the rusty yellow one. She looked down at herself and saw she was once again wearing the little black dress from the hotel lobby. Instead of the high heels, however, this time the shoes were more sensible.

"Now, do not forget." Belent's voice came from beside her but was quickly interrupted by Zander.

"I know, working it now." Again, the handsome face tightened, and Rey watched jewels appear on her wrists and fingers, and a black watch winked into existence on Zander's arm. "Remember where we parked," Zander said with a smile as the vehicle came to a stop.

There were now ten cars in the lot, and she hoped the inside wasn't too busy. As they climbed the gray steps up to the front doors, Rey took a deep breath and said a silent prayer to the goddess.

The inside of the building was quite impressive. It reminded her a little of the library in Denver, except cozier. Stairs ran up the right side of the building and there were several levels of floors that rose above them. There was a security desk directly in front of them and behind that a door opened to an office.

"Ah, here we go," Zander whispered. He guided her to the desk.

"Can I help you?" The security woman wore a dark uniform, but Rey didn't see any weapon and let out a small breath of relief.

"Yes, we would like to speak to the curator," Zander said with a charming smile.

"I'm afraid he isn't available at this time." The woman smiled. Her eyes never left Zander. Rey saw him increase his charm and smile as he leaned forward a little over the desk.

"Ah, Agnes, is it?" he said, reading her clearly marked name tag. "I have a special donation and wanted to do a spot check to see if your museum is where I want my pieces to be displayed."

Rey knew what to look for, but still, she almost missed Belent's blue magic race toward the woman. The lady's brown eyes turned hazy for a second, then she stood and nodded, a slightly goofy smile on her lips.

"I see, yes, please follow me." Agnes walked them towards the door and beyond to a small hallway. Four doors led off the hallway. Two went to empty offices, while the other held a small kitchen. They walked to the last door and stopped.

"Mr. Colby, I have a..." Agnes turned to study Zander, who quickly spoke up.

"Mr. and Mrs. Haddock," Zander supplied with a smile.

Mr. Colby, a rather small pale man, glanced up from behind a large wooden desk and stared openly at them. Rey gave a small smile when his beady eyes glanced at her jewels, and her smile widened when he nodded once to her.

"I have no appointments today, Agnes," Mr. Colby said sternly.

"Ah, yes, we do apologize, but my wife here was quite insistent that we stop by your little museum today. She wanted to see the layout before we confirmed our rather large donation of rare items." Zander stepped forward with a smile. "I know we should have scheduled something, but this trip was quite unexpected."

"Ah, Mr. Haddock?" Mr. Colby asked as he stood and surveyed them. After a stern look to his security, Agnes left them to return to her post.

"Yes, I am sorry. I told my wife it would be quite rude to just stop by, but you know women, once they get something in their mind." Zander drew Rey in for a side hug as she tried not to glare at him.

"Yes, well, please have a seat." Mr. Colby gestured to the chairs in front of his desk.

"Actually, we were wondering if you could give us a tour first. Quite a busy schedule," Zander replied. "We only have a few minutes to look over your facilities."

"Ah." Mr. Colby looked hesitantly at them.

"Of course, I will need your information and there will be follow-up meetings, that is if the building agrees with us. Our sizable donation will require quite a bit of space, and the money..." Zander trailed off and they watched Mr. Colby's bushy eyebrows raise half an inch.

"Why, yes, of course," he quickly interjected. He almost tripped over his own shoes as he led them out of his office and back into the main entrance hall.

They were shown the main floor's entrance and told all about the building and its architectural highlights. He then explained about their vast number of displays, which contained several unique and engaging pieces of art.

As they climbed the stairs, Rey knew that Belent would be using his magic to pinpoint the object they would need to return home. Zander kept the curator busy with questions or polite comments as they drew upwards. Paintings and pottery filled the stairway and hallways. Art filled the rooms off to either side of the walkway.

"The Bistro is a great place for lunch, and we often host events there too," Mr. Colby explained with pride.

Rey felt Belent brush against her arm as they neared the next floor. Turning, she noticed a sign that said 'American Indian Art.'

"Can we view this area?" she asked innocently.

With a quick nod, Zander smoothly steered Mr. Colby into the room as he continued his conversation about the building's open space.

The room they entered was more expansive than the entry hall. Wooden floors and white walls gave an open feeling, and hidden lights shone down upon hundreds of objects hidden behind glass cubes.

The items, Rey thought, reminded her of home. There were handwoven baskets much like the ones her tribe used along the Cliffs of Faro. Purses and leather clothing were displayed, and she even saw a fake horse. It was a small creature the color of sand, nothing like the vibrant colors of her home's horses.

There were several pictures and even some woven rugs on display that drew her attention. Zander and Mr. Colby were slowly walking about the room while she remained just inside the doorway.

There was a small family of three off to their left. A woman, man, and a teenage boy were busy studying the horse as they read a brass plaque near its base. None of them gave any notice to the new arrivals.

"Hurry," she whispered, hoping Belent could hear her as Zander guided Mr. Colby over to one corner and asked about an object in an attempt to distract the man.

"There," Belent whispered in her ear. "That glass cases in the corner. It's in there, the long ax."

"Cats." Rey studied the case. The thick glass had no apparent opening or latches. "We didn't think about getting it out."

Zander kept the curator of the little museum distracted by asking question about the building, the exhibits, and even the town. However, he himself kept his eyes on Rey as he tried to listen for any sound from Belent.

He noticed when Rey went stiff and saw her nod her chin in the direction of a small glass case. After giving the case a quick look, he assumed that his two friends were currently panicking about how to get the item out from behind the thick glass. But Zander had kept this part of his plan to himself. Until now...

He knew craftiness was needed. He also understood that they would need to steal the object. That required stealth, something neither of his friends understood.

Rey was a warrior. Her idea of stealth was to walk in the front door, exclaim her intentions, and demand compliance. If that didn't work, then she would fight to get her way, usually using her hard and powerful right hook.

Belent was another matter. The sorcerer had been using his magic for so long now. His idea of a plan was to encase the whole museum within his magic. Then he would boldly walk in, take what he wanted, and leave everyone in confusion as to what had happened.

Zander was worried that both Rey's and Belent's plans would draw the attention of General Wilberg.

"Mr. Colby, what happened there?" Zander asked as he threw his magic towards the case in question. In a flash, his magic made it look like the glass had disappeared. To Mr. Colby, the case now sat uncovered and opened.

"What in heaven's name?" Mr. Colby quickly ran over to the display.

"Have you been robbed?" Zander innocently asked as

he gently pulled the small key chain off the man's belt. He had first spotted the keys hanging from the man's belt while in the offices down on the main floor.

Zander knew he was gambling and hoped the chain held the key to this display. If it didn't, he had a backup plan that involved smashing the glass.

"Where is the glass?" Mr. Colby asked, his gray eyes wide with confusion as he leaned over the invisible case.

"Is anything missing?" Zander asked, quickly and silently waving to his friends.

"I..." Mr. Colby started but then moved to look at each item that was located in the case as Rey and Belent drew near.

Belent whispered in Zander's ear the details of the item, and Zander saw a rather odd-looking ax. It had leather wrapped around its wooden handle and two white feathers with a charm near its blade. The blade was made of stone and no bigger than his hand.

He gave his friends a nod, then changed his magic so Mr. Colby could no longer see the ax sitting in its current resting place. Once it went invisible, he focused harder and moved closer to the small man, who was now almost doubled over above the case.

"The Chief's tomahawk is missing," Mr. Colby finally exclaimed, panic in is voice as he quickly reached in his pocket and pulled out a little black square. After he pushed a few buttons, they all heard a ringing coming from the device.

"Pick up the phone," Mr. Colby said, sounding agitated.

Finally, they heard Agnes' voice come out of the little box.

"Hello?"

"Agnes, shut down the building. There has been a break-in," Mr. Colby exclaimed.

Panic wanted to set in, but Zander kept his cool as he felt Belent take the keys from his hand. They immediately disappeared.

Mr. Colby was oblivious to this act as he continued to talk into the phone. The man sputtered to Agnes as he spun around on the spot, as if he expected the thief and ax to just magically appear.

Zander felt an odd thumping in his chest and worried there were security measures that they didn't know or understand. But as the air grew quiet again, he waited with his magic active until he felt Belent's hand rest upon his arm. He nodded once and pulled his invisibility magic from the glass just as Agnes and another security guard came into the room.

"Hurry. Have you closed and locked all the doors?" Mr. Colby demanded as she approached.

"Sir, yes. But what is missing?" she asked. She drew near as Mr. Colby pointed towards the display case, where the glass had now reappeared, along with the tomahawk, which magically sat once again on the white linen inside the case.

"What?" Mr. Colby stuttered as he drew near. Zander had a quick second to clip the keys back on the man's belt before he reached for them. "What? It was gone. The glass and the tomahawk, they were both missing."

Agnes looked doubtfully at the little curator as he quickly found the key that unlocked the display case. After lifting the thick glass, he reached for the object, and Zander had to focus hard on the illusion to give it the feel of substance.

"I don't understand," Mr. Colby stated as Agnes shook

her head again and looked at the man with concern written on her face.

"Did you have breakfast this morning? Remember your blood pressure." She clucked her tongue at him. "Maybe you need a snack, or maybe a vacation?"

"Yes," Mr. Colby answered absentmindedly as he set the illusional ax back in the case and closed it, then resecured the lock.

"I think we should head to our next appointment," Rey said, shaking her head at the curator. "I hope you feel better soon," she added as Zander drew her towards the doors with a nod.

They were two flights down when Agnes came up from behind them. She was filled with apologies about her boss. Once she saw them outside, they quickly walked to their vehicle.

Zander kept his magic active all the way there. He focused hard as they drove out of the parking lot. He worried that Corbin would have to drive for a while, as he was getting a headache from concentrating.

Belent finally reappeared next to Rey in the vehicle. They had just turned down the paved lane that would lead them back to the small town when Rey let out a quick gasp.

"Cats!" Belent hissed as Zander slammed on the brakes of the car, causing it to skid sideways in the road before it finally came to a halt.

Blocking the road back to the town where their friends were hiding sat the military trucks of General Wilberg.

10

PRISONER'S WOE

Rey could still feel Belent sitting next to her in the truck, but the sorcerer was invisible to any eyes, including any video cameras.

The massive army was blocking the road, keeping them from their friends, who were still in the town several miles away, and from escape.

"What do we do?" she asked as she studied the army of men in dark green and brown uniforms. Each man was pointing an odd black stick at them. Four flying machines hovered behind the blockage, emitting odd whomping sounds that could be heard and felt. These flying machines weren't as big as the dragons from her world, but they were impressive to see.

"Caution is needed here," Belent warned from beside her.

"Stay with us if you can. Then get back to the others and formulate a rescue plan," Zander warned as he leaned back in defeat and lifted his magic, which immediately changed the image of the car back to the old yellow truck.

"What are you saying?" Rey felt panic set in as he turned the truck off then lifted his hands in surrender. "Let's fight," she hissed, and he shook his head.

"No. I know they don't look dangerous, but those are guns. Remember in the movies we watched?" Rey thought back to the movies Zander and Corbin had watched while stuck in the hotel. The guns had been in almost all of them and, besides making a loud noise, were reportedly responsible for puncturing the body with a projectile. "This means we get captured," he stated.

She sucked in a quick breath and glared out the window at the advancing men. Wishing for her dragon and fellow warriors from home, she too raised her hands in defeat.

"Careful," Zander warned and gave her a stern look. "We may lose today, but our friends are still free to aid us."

"Fine." She pouted as Belent quickly opened the door and slipped out before she herself climbed out of the truck. Zander quickly followed.

What proceeded next was nothing short of abuse and filled with embarrassing moments. In the end, she, a dragon warrior, was left shackled and feeling helpless. The attacking men used thick leather gloves to handle her and Zander. Their arms were forced behind them, and they were shoved to the ground.

A knee rammed into the small of her back, and she had to grit her teeth to hold back her impulse to fight. She heard Zander grunt and before she could look over at him, a black sack was slapped down over her head, completely blocking out any light.

Tousled, shoved, and jumbled around, she was finally thrown against a hard metal object. She felt her chained hands being clasped to something else. After a few moments, the truck she was in started to move. No words were spoken to her, and she worried that Zander and she were being taken to different places.

"Zander?" she asked, angered by the fear in her voice.

"I'm here," he replied, and she quickly took a breath of relief. "Stay calm," he said, and she took comfort in the apparent calm in his voice.

"Where are you taking us?" she demanded, but no answer came, and she wondered if they had been left alone inside the truck.

They rode in silence for several minutes before they stopped moving and their captors pulled them out. She was forced to walk at a quick pace and felt a man on either side of her, each carrying her more than letting her walk.

When she felt the soft ground below her turn solid, she guessed they were inside a building. She was forced to sit, and then once again felt them chain her hands to something solid. The bag on her head was ripped off.

When she didn't see Zander, her panic wanted to rise once again. She was in a small tent with dark green walls. A metal table sat between her, and the man Zander had called General Wilberg. He was a man of middle age, and his hair, which was cut very short, had already gone pure white. Wrinkles lined his face, particularly around his brown eyes, which studied her intently.

"Hello," she said. She leaned back in her chair as he continued to study her. "What's going on?" she asked sweetly.

"Where is she?" came the man's response.

"She?" Rey asked, genuinely perplexed.

"The one called Anna. Where has she gone?" The question was more a command and, when she didn't answer, he leaned forward a little. "Where do you come from?"

"Ah, well that is an interesting story," Rey said seriously. "I grew up on the cliffs by the ocean. Love it there. My family has been there for over four generations." She saw anger creep into the man's eyes. "Of course, now I'm landlocked, but the forest is just as interesting and very nice."

"Where?" the man demanded, slamming his fist on the table. "What planet?"

She looked at him as if he had grown a second head and said nothing, hoping her reaction was convincing.

"Where are the others? How did you and the others escape before? What form of magic did you use?" he demanded.

She laughed, and General Wilberg quickly stood and leaned towards her.

"Look, I didn't do any magic," she insisted, knowing the truth was stretched thin here. "I don't know anything about it."

"The car. We saw it turn back into the stolen truck," the general advised as he returned to his seat. "If you didn't do the magic, then it must be your companion." Fear leaped into her and before she could hide it, she saw the man smile slightly. "Ah, it was him."

With this, the sack was thrust back on her head, and she was once again forced to march between the two men.

She felt the soft ground beneath her feet for a few minutes, then she was unceremoniously thrown onto hard ground. Her hands were still secured behind her, and the sack had been left on her head. When she heard a door shut and then the click of a lock, she guessed she had finally been left alone, imprisoned.

It took some time and a lot of wiggling to get the sack off

her head. When it finally slipped off, she saw that she was in a small metal room. The walls were slatted in evenly spaced rows, all a dirty brown. The ceiling and floor were made from the same material but were missing the odd rows.

With a little wiggling, she soon was facing the massive double-wide doors. She was discouraged when she could hear movement beyond and guessed there were plenty of guards outside.

Glancing down, she noticed in the faint light that came from small cracks around the doors that her clothing was filthy. What rust or dirt had been on the floor now covered her completely. Kicking up her legs, she widened her arms and easily slipped her feet through them, successfully bringing her hands to her front.

Metal clasps linked her wrists together and she wondered for a moment if she could unlock them. There was a small keyhole, but she didn't know if she had any of her possessions still.

Feeling her pockets, she realized that all of her weapons were missing. When she felt the tiny birthday gift Charlotte had given her, she was shocked and pleased. She pulled it from her pocket and studied the simple brown wrapping.

Finally shaking her head, she felt her other pockets and found only a single hair band, two slips of paper, and one of Zander's candy bars.

Frustrated, she decided to open the gift to see if the box held anything she could use to free herself. Her frustration was quickly forgotten when she saw the present Princess Charlotte had given her.

"Cats." She studied the pretty trinket inside. She fingered the carved image of a flying swan, its neck delicately curved. She was studying the leather strap as several loud pops came from just outside her prison door. They were followed closely by screams.

The sudden noise caused her to struggle even harder against her bonds.

Zander sat chained to the chair, his back straight, as his anger built inside him.

Time slowly ticked by, and nothing happened. He flexed his arms and felt the hard cold steel bite into his wrists, cutting his skin and bringing more anger to the front.

General Wilberg.

His mother's nemesis here on Earth. The man was still alive and still causing trouble. But Zander wondered how this man could still be alive.

Everything Zander's mother had told him about Earth had spoken of time being different on the two planets. Surely time hadn't gone so slowly on Earth that the man was still alive.

His mother had always told her children the wonders of Earth, both fantasy stories told on Earth and the real events she had lived through.

Zander believed that over forty years must have passed here on Earth since his mother had escaped in a red sports car with Wizard Leian. If this was the case, then the man who had just captured him was well over eighty.

He gave his wrists another flex and then heard someone shuffle next to him. He assumed it was the guards set to watch him. He still wore the damned hood that blocked out all light but was thankful he could still hear and smell. One guard smelled like bacon, the other like sour milk, which caused Zander to admire one while detesting the other.

"So," a deep voice said, and Zander understood that the general had finally joined him in the holding room he had been sitting in.

When the hood was finally ripped off his head, Zander stared at the man, hate filling his eyes. A metal table sat between them in a dimly lit room with a single electrical light sitting upon it.

Glancing up, Zander noticed cameras and TV screens lined one wall. This added to his frustration. His magic wouldn't work here.

"Six nights ago, there was an escape. A woman called Anna," the general stated as he sat behind the table and set a stack of pages on the table before him.

"Six?" Zander blurted out before he could stop himself. Six nights? What was this man talking about? Six nights ago, Zander had been in Denver, but his mother had been back on Genoa, or wherever she and his dad had been whisked to by the evil red mist.

"In Boston. I had tracked her there and a blond man, not you by the way, took her away in a red Mustang convertible." He proceeded to list a license plate and the details, including the year of the car. Then he sat and stared at Zander. "That car has not been found yet."

"Good luck with that," Zander said with a smirk.

He knew exactly where the car was—outside the wizard's town of Tharian, still sitting against the large tree next to the magical portal called the Orick.

He knew this because he and Corbin had snuck away one day and found the car after hearing stories of it. They hadn't been able to get the car started but had studied it in detail.

"If you know of the car, then you must know of the woman," General Wilberg stated as he shuffled the papers. "Where is she?"

"That is a great question," Zander said with a big sigh. Then he sat silently as he studied the man. Was this man correct? Had he come to Earth days before his mother had actually been rescued from this planet? He set these questions aside and promised he would ask Belent when he got a chance.

"The escape from Denver—there were three others we had captured there. Where are they and how did you instigate their escape?" When Zander only sat and stared at him, the general continued. "What magic did you use?"

Again silence.

"The other, she said—" This was all the general got out before Zander strained against his chains.

"Rey. Where is she?" he demanded as he tried to break his bonds. His arm muscles flexed against his bonds.

"Ah, her name is Rey," the general stated calmly. He took a pen from his breast pocket and wrote something on the top page. "Any last name?" When he was met with silence, he nodded and set the pen down. "The magic," he continued. "Where did you acquire this?"

Silence.

"The one called Anna. We have records that she was born that way. Were you born with it?" he asked.

Again silence.

"Where were you born?"

Zander squinted his eyes and looked bored.

"Where do you come from?" The general's eyes

narrowed, and Zander could hear a hint of frustration in his tone.

"Over the rainbow," Zander murmured, but this answer seemed to fascinate the general.

"Ah, another place. Maybe another world?" The general nodded. "How did you get here?"

"I traveled here in a car," Zander said with another smile as Wilberg narrowed his own eyes.

"You look like her," the man said quite suddenly, which shocked Zander. When the general leaned forward to study him better, Zander tilted back in his own chair. "Did she tell you I knew her for a long time. I knew her and the man called Orden."

Zander had heard the stories; he knew everything about the general and his obsession with hunting his mother. He knew this man, and the army he led, would imprison him and his friends for years while trying to find out their secrets. He also knew that eventually they would kill and dissect them, all in the name of science.

"The truck. Tell me how it was transformed," the general asked quite suddenly.

He remained silent and saw another hint of frustration build in the older man's eyes, which made him smile.

"I know it was you that worked the magic. Tell me, do you have to touch the object to change it?" Before the question was finished there was a shout outside the room, followed quickly by several loud bang, which Zander guessed were shots from a gun.

"What is that?" the general demanded. He waved his hand, and the bag was once again pushed over Zander's head.

Zander felt panic set in as worry for his friends

increased. Were they shooting at Rey? Had she tried to escape? Was she hurt?

Just the thought of her injured had his knees going weak with fear. He tried to see or hear anything that would help him discover the answers to his questions.

He heard what sounded like several men running just outside the room and then a car engine revving up. Off in the distance he heard the flying machine start up and felt the odd thumping of its massive blades. Finally, the odd sound dimmed after the machine took off and moved away from his prison.

He was left alone several more minutes, and time seemed to stop.

Frustrated at his lack of control, lack of freedom, he chewed on the inside of his mouth and tried his bonds once again. He felt blood seep from his left wrist, where the metal dug into his flesh.

The following silence almost drove him into despair. His imagination drew up several scenarios, all of which resulted in Rey dying. His anger built and once again he felt the bite of steel against his blood.

What seemed like hours later, he finally heard the sound of boots, another slam of a door, and a soft hissing noise before more silence.

"Close the gates. Ensure the other one is still locked up, then go into defense mode." The general's calm voice came closer.

Zander took a breath of relief at the man's words. It meant that it wasn't Rey they were hunting. He thought quickly of Belent, and his worry came back.

If the sorcerer had been discovered and captured, then the others would never know where they were. His friends, who were still hidden in the small town, would never know what had happened to them. They might be searching for them and wander right into the army.

The hood was once more removed from Zander's head. General Wilberg stood before him.

"Now, tell me where the others are."

11

FREEDOM'S WOE

Corbin watched his best friend and crown prince disappear down the road in the stolen truck and winced inwardly.

Here he was, a freedom fighter by birth, hiding and avoiding the risks. Risks that he was born to take, a trait embedded in him by his mother and father.

Corbin had been raised within the ranks of the freedom fighters who now served the king of Matera. Corbin's father was also the best friend of the king of Genoa. This meant that Corbin had spent his childhood much like Zander, traveling all over Genoa.

Some of his childhood had been spent down in Matera. His grandmother still ran an inn outside of Pesha, and he had several cousins who lived there still.

Other times he would travel with Zander's family. The cliffs were his favorite, although he enjoyed Castle Pines because that's usually where his best friend was.

It was in Castle Pines that he had met the love of his life, Avaline. Corbin had been transfixed with the blond warrior since he had first laid eyes on her. She, however, hadn't felt the same at first.

It had taken him several weeks to win the lady over, and then they had started courting. But she too was a trained warrior and their duties had kept them apart most of the year, she along the cliffs with her tribe and he always going where his friend the prince went.

Except now. Now on Earth he found himself left behind. Shaking his head, he turned to study the large group behind him.

"Well, friends, let's see if we can move this trip along," he stated. He studied Avaline. Her clear gray eyes studied him skeptically, and she pulled a lock of hair back behind her ear and then set her hand on her right hip. She was a beauty and, after giving her a wink, he reached for her hand.

"Please tell me you are not going to disobey orders," she demanded as a frown formed on her full lips.

"Of course not," Corbin said with a wicked grin, a grin most would have said mirrored his best friend's. "He never said anything about acquiring a vehicle and following at a safe distance. He just said if they didn't return by nightfall to make for the falls. And we will do that when it gets dark."

Corbin saw Seth nod once and then the older man took off down the small street, no doubt looking for a replacement truck.

"Sash, how about you and Mateo go find supplies. Use the card thingy that Belent left with us to buy some." Corbin smiled as he looked down the street at the small town. "Reminds me of Pesha a little," he murmured, smiling when he spotted a post office hardly bigger than the double doors leading into it.

"What can we do?" Mika asked as she and Leon stepped forward.

"Well, if all goes right, we will need to know how to get to the falls. Can you two study the map and memorize the path?" Corbin turned and saw Kylo and the others step forward. "I won't know what else we need until after we get a truck."

The truck turned out to be a van, and they didn't even need to steal it. Seth returned with a wide smile, keys, and a story.

"The man said he had never seen a sword like mine," Seth said with a shake of his head. "Traded the van, a full tank of gas, and some sandwiches all for my sword."

"I'll make sure yours is replaced," Corbin stated as he slapped Seth on his back.

The van smelled of must and old cigarettes, but it started, and they all fit in it very comfortably. Corbin was excited to drive, and he took a few minutes getting familiar with the controls. Then he had Kenzo sit behind the wheel to let him learn how to drive the machine too. It would be better if several of them knew how to drive.

Before Sash and Mateo returned with supplies, Kenzo had driven several circles in the parking lot, a wide smile on his dark face and his slanted eyes wide with amusement.

"Good, now we have another driver just in case," Corbin said as the supplies were packed into the van. "Now, let's go slowly up the road to take a peek at the museum."

There were two roads to the museum. Corbin knew his three friends had taken the main road, and if all worked out, that would be the road they would return by. But he wanted a peek up the road to ensure they would safely return.

Normally, Corbin wasn't a very patient man, and when

it came to Zander, he would have rather died than see his friend harmed. Loyalty ran deep in his family, and in him.

He let Kenzo drive but gave him the directions that would take them down the single lane road. Trees lines this road, but only on one side. The other was open to vast fields of tall wheat.

"They might be done by now," Avaline said, worry in her voice as she leaned over Corbin from the back passenger seat.

"Maybe. If so, they will get to the town safely and wait for us." He looked out the window. He had just heard something that bothered him. It reminded him of one of the helicopters he had seen in the war movies the other night.

When he saw the black machine dart out of the sky to their left, he hissed at Kenzo to pull over underneath a patch of trees on the side of the road.

"What is it?" Kenzo asked as he too leaned far forward to study the sky.

Another helicopter flew past and then a third, all black as night, and panic filled Corbin.

"Trouble," Corbin said with a shake of his head.

He watched the machines line up and head to their right. Dust rose from that direction, and he quickly asked for the map. After studying it for a minute, he nodded as dread filled him.

"They head to the main road. I think it's a trap," he informed the others.

"What do we do?" Seth asked from the back of the van.

"Depends." He turned to study the others.

"On what?" Seth asked, his face grimly set.

"On if you are good at following orders or not," Corbin said with an ominous smile. "Me? I'm horrible at following them."

They left the van there, while most of them stayed back, including Kenzo, who was the only other warrior who could drive. Corbin took Sash, hoping the large warrior could contend with some of Earth's military men, remembering the hard time Sash had given the men in Denver. He also brought Kylo, who was almost as big as Sash; Avaline, whose knives were more wicked than anything he had ever seen; and Mateo, who was a skilled tracker.

They traveled light, as their mission wasn't to engage in a rescue but to do reconnaissance only. The others would remain in the van and wait for their return until dark, then would proceed north to Fairy Falls and seek help from the other Belent found there.

Corbin hoped they would get to the museum before their friends were captured but doubted it. As they walked stealthily through the rolling fields that surrounded the building, his doubts increased. He had a gut feeling that he would not get to Zander before the military did.

They crested the last hill before the main road and dropped to their bellies when they were confronted by the horrific sight of the military lined up before them.

"Cats!" Kylo swore as they saw their friends being handcuffed and marched into a waiting truck. The enemy numbered more than fifty, all armed and all dressed in the same uniform.

Mateo pushed forward a little and tugged on Corbin's sleeve. "Look." His pale eyes looked off to their left. "That one vehicle, see the men."

Corbin turned and saw a single vehicle standing several yards off from the main group. The jeep had a flat tire, and two men were bent over, in the process of changing it. Both were of medium build. One had a hat covering his head, while the other had dark black hair cut short.

Turning, Corbin studied his friends and gaged that Mateo had a build most similar to one of the men down at the jeep. He turned back and studied the other military man and realized that he had a similar build to him.

"I see," Corbin stated and turned to address his friends. "Well, looks like Mateo and I are going on an adventure. Return to the others and follow as best you can."

"Just what do you think you are doing?" Avaline demanded from the other side of him, a deep frown on her face and her gray eyes narrowed to slits.

"There's only two of them. We'll overthrow them and take their uniforms," Corbin stated as he turned to look at her. "Then we'll follow the army to where they have our people. Once there, we can figure out how to free them."

"Or get killed." She frowned and shook her head.

"If we can't free them, we'll escape and return to the town before the sun rises tomorrow," he insisted, running a finger along her cheek.

"Better leave your packs here," Sash stated quietly and slid over to take Corbin's weapons from him.

"Look, the rest are driving past the jeep," Mateo informed them as he handed his weapons to Avaline. "We better go now."

Corbin planted a solid kiss on Aveline's lips. Then with a smile, he took off at a run behind the tracker towards the jeep and adventure.

Corbin was having a blast!

He and Mateo had easily overpowered the two military men. They had stripped them of their uniforms and quickly dressed in them. Each fit nicely if a bit too snug around the crotch for Corbin's liking.

He was thankful the men had finished fixing the tire before they had attacked them. He wasn't sure he could have done the repairs in time to follow the other vehicles, which were now miles ahead.

He was also thankful the helicopters were flying above the procession. All he had to do was aim the jeep in that direction. Within miles, he saw the dust of the military trucks.

They drove for fifteen miles, at one point going up and over a mountain. The air grew cold, homes grew sparse, and the forest grew thick around the narrow road. The road twisted and curved, and then they finally turned onto a small dirt trail that immediately turned back on itself and then shot out of the forest into a vast field.

Another fifteen minutes of slow travel over rocks and dirt ruts had them approaching a temporary fence guarded by military men dressed similar to themselves now.

"Well, it's now or never," Corbin said. Mateo nodded and leaned forward a little as they hit a bump.

"I'm just glad it's getting dark," his friend said as they neared the main gate.

"Papers," came the order as Corbin rolled the window down and handed him the two identifications. They had been lucky. The men they had 'replaced' had similar features to them. The only difference was Corbin's bright red hair, but he had quickly tucked it under the man's hat.

"Foods in the mess hall to the left." This was the only response they got as they were waved forward without a second glance.

Corbin took a huge breath in relief as he drove away. He looked back in the mirror and sent a big thank-you to the goddess for their luck. He found a parking spot, and before they left the safety of the car, they had their plan set.

"We need to find the others," he said to Mateo, who nodded his pale head. "But we also need a means to escape this compound."

"You find our friends; I'll secure an exit," Mateo said. The man flashed a bright smile before he exited the car.

"Meet back here. Give a whistle if it's not safe." Corbin took a minute and studied his surroundings before he too left the safety of the car.

Driving around the compound had been easy. The tents sat in grids. There were wide lanes between the rows for cars to travel down. There were three large tents in the center and four odd-looking metal boxes directly behind the center tent. Knowing his friends wouldn't be kept prisoners easily, he immediately aimed for the metal boxes.

He got about ten feet away from the first box when he met with his first obstacle. There were very bright lights lined all around the boxes that would point out anyone sneaking about.

The second obstacle was that there were guards. Five large men stood outside one of the boxes, their long, odd guns held in their arms and their eyes scanning the darkness beyond.

One good thing about the guards being there was that Corbin no longer had to search for his missing friends. He knew that the first box held at least one of his companions. At the moment, none of the other boxes were being guarded.

Staying hidden in the dark, he took several minutes to

study the lights and prison boxes. Then he turned on his heels and continued to survey the encampment.

He found the mess hall. The smells of food drifted out to him, and his stomach complained loudly. He saw several men entering another tent and stopped just outside that tent's back wall and listened for a while.

"Don't understand the orders," came one deep voice.

"Not our place to understand, just follow," someone replied.

"Aren't we infringing upon their rights?" a higher voice asked.

"I don't think the general cares," the second voice responded again.

"He's been crazy since the girl slipped away."

"How did she do that?" the high voice asked.

"Don't know. Probably mirrors or something," the first voice stated.

"So, who are these two?" asked the high voice.

"Don't know, but I would hate to be them," deep voice stated.

"Girl's a looker," one said.

"I can't wait for my shift change and a chance to watch her, if you know what I mean," the deep voice said with a laugh.

This gave Corbin an idea, but he stayed and listened to more of their conversation before he moved on.

He had just rounded the back side of another tent when he felt a hand clasp over his mouth.

"Shh." Corbin heard the sorcerer's voice right next to his ear and relaxed. "It's me."

"I know." He moved to shrug the hand off of him and discovered that he couldn't actually see the hand, nor the sorcerer. "Where in the king's name are you?"

"Right in front of you," Belent replied. "I am invisible."

"I wasn't born yesterday. Tell me, do you have a plan?" Corbin asked, thankful Belent was there to aid in the rescue.

"Not yet. Are you alone?" Belent asked.

"Mateo is about. He's securing means to escape." Corbin turned back to study the high lights that surrounded his friends' prison.

"I have an idea, but we need the escape route first," Corbin said with a smile. "And one of those cool guns."

Twenty minutes later, the three from Genoa huddled behind the tent closest to the boxes. Belent had insisted on remaining invisible, but Mateo and Corbin didn't mind. Corbin thought it was the coolest thing and, since the sorcerer had procured the gun, he thought it was a good idea.

"The new truck is just behind that tent," Mateo said, pointing to their left. "Keys are in it, and the back is empty."

"What about the diversion?" Belent asked.

"Already set. You said you can detonate from here?" Corbin asked.

"Yes, but you are sure no one is near it?" Belent asked. "I will not kill just to free our friends."

"Yes, yes, you said that. It's set on the surrounding fence. The guards aren't posted there, only at the gates," Corbin advised. He bent over the gun to study it.

"Don't point that at me," Mateo hissed. He shoved the object away from his midsection.

"Sorry. I know there's a safety, but I can't find it." Corbin grinned when he finally found it. "Here. Ok, once I have the first light out, we can—"

"No, don't shoot each one. That will take skill and time. Here, see that long thick rope?" Belent said. The men reminded him that he was invisible, and they couldn't see where he was pointing. "There, on the ground, see how it connects each light? Shoot that, then all the lights will go dark."

Corbin nodded and aimed, hoping the guns were easy to aim or at least similar to a bow. His first shot was ten feet off. He quickly adjusted and after two more quick tries, the lights finally went out.

But by then, the whole camp was in chaos.

12

THINGS THAT SPARKLE

Rey's worry turned to panic when the faint light in her prison went out. Her fingers quickly wrapped protectively around the swan bracelet, and she felt her bonds instantly fall away from her wrists.

"What?" How in the world had that happened? It seemed like magic, but she couldn't do magic. She wondered if Belent were nearby. But that seemed too good to be true. She looked at the bracelet in her hand and shook her head. She didn't have time to think about it right now. If her friends were behind the sounds outside, then she needed to let them know where she was.

She could hear the guards outside shouting orders, but the gunfire had gone quiet. She was thankful for this, as the sound set a deep fear inside her. She too had watched the movies, and the idea of guns frightened her. Give her a sharp sword or even a bow and she was a fierce warrior, but the idea of being shot from a far distance scared her to her core.

"I'm in here," she screamed, banging her fists against the

door. The minute her fist hit the first door, the latches released and both heavy metal doors flew open. "What is going on?" she exclaimed, but then she was immediately faced with two large guards.

"How did you do that?" the first guard asked, raising his gun at her.

Rey quickly crouched and kicked his feet out from under him. Then she planted her left elbow in his face, knocking him out.

She spun and stood. Soon, the second guard was on his back after a swift hard kick in his privates. She turned quickly and was just about to dispatch a third guard when she saw his bright red hair in the faint light and paused.

"Corbin?" She rushed forward, relief filling her when she saw it was her friend instead of the enemy.

"Hey, Rey. We heard you might need some help," Corbin said with a smile. "Where's Zander?"

"Hurry," Belent's voice came. To her shock, Corbin nodded and quickly lifted her over his shoulders and ran away from her prison at a fast pace.

"No, we need to get Zander," she cried as her long hair blew into her face as she hung upside down along Corbin's back.

"All part of the plan," Corbin replied with a grunt as he raced away from the commotion.

She was thrown unceremoniously into the back of a truck and let out a few choice words about Corbin. She tried to scramble to her feet.

"Not yet, princess," Corbin said and shoved her back down. "Get in here and stay," he demanded and once again she found herself imprisoned in a dark box. "Stay there until one of us gets you."

Frustrated, and not wanting to hide during a fight, she tried to find a more comfortable position. The box was at least a foot shorter than she was, but the side walls gave her arms room to move about. It had an odd metallic smell and reminded her of the back of the truck they had traveled there in.

She wondered what the sorcerer and Corbin were up to, what plan they had made. And, most importantly, were they going to be able to free Zander?

It felt like hours before she heard an engine start and her box started to shake and rumble to life. When her world gave a quick jerk, she muffled a shriek and strained her ears to listen. Her box bounced around with her inside. Her head hit the lid and her left elbow rapped hard against the side as she was thrown about.

Were her friends there? Where was Zander? Where were Belent and Corbin? Were they the ones driving the truck that she was hiding in?

Unwilling to give up her hiding place without a weapon, she tried to see something beyond her secure box, but couldn't. She tried the lid finally and found it securely latched, locking her in.

Panic wanted to take a hold inside her, but she bit her lower lip once and tried giving the lid a harder shove. Still nothing.

Pouting a little, she wiggled a little in her box and tried pushing again. When the truck gave a huge lurch, she muffled another scream as she was thrown to the side.

She felt the truck hit a smooth road and the jarring ride smoothed out briefly, but then the truck took a sharp turn, and she once again found herself bouncing around inside her small box.

After her face had hit the top of the box, she braced herself with her arms and feet and used all her strength to keep herself from bashing against the box's walls.

By the time the truck stopped, her arms and legs were shaking with fatigue. She was bruised and scraped and dirty. She hoped it was her friends driving the truck and feared they might not be far enough from the general.

Several minutes passed and her frustration grew when the truck started once more. She thought briefly of pounding her fists against the walls of her box, but she still feared she was surrounded by the military men from Earth.

More twists and turns caused her to lose track of any direction. For all she knew, she could be on her way back to the encampment. Back to her prison.

This thought had a new panic rising in her, and she took a few deep breaths to calm herself.

After a while the ride became smoother again, and she no longer had to brace her legs and arms against the box's sides.

When she awoke, shocked she had been asleep, it was to find the lid to her box was slowly opening. Her muscles were cramped and tight from the restriction, but she still leaped up from her position with startling ease.

"Whoa," came Zander's shocked voice. Relief filled her. "Easy," he urged as she rushed into his arms.

"They got you out too," she exclaimed as she fought the tears in her eyes and tried to stop her arms from shaking.

"Hey now." Zander's voice sounded shocked then panicked as he squeezed her tight. "Of course. Belent and Mateo, well... I'll tell you later," he said.

She pushed away from him and stared at him hard. Her anger quickly replaced her worry, and she squinted her eyes at him. Standing with her feet still inside her box, she placed both her hands on her hips and glared at him.

"What happened? Why was I stuck in that box so long?" She saw Zander's face pink a little and her eyes narrowed even more.

"Well, it wasn't my plan," he quickly said, looking around the back of the covered truck. "But I will tell you after we get cleaned up. Come, I think there's food in the house." He helped her the rest of the way out of her box.

"House?" she asked. She followed him, her hand still in his.

The house was small, but it was safe.

Zander led Rey inside the wooden structure. The rest of the band followed, and soon everyone was sitting around two small tables. Within the hour, there were piles of food on the plates and bowls set in front of them. The aroma of cooked meat and spices filled the air, and Rey's stomach rumbled loudly.

He tried not to laugh at her discomfort, for he still felt bad that she'd had to ride all the way inside the box, hidden from eyes, until their arrival. He helped her find a seat and pushed Leon out of the chair next to her and took his place. Then he gave Rey a wide smile.

"Welcome," a dark-haired woman said from the corner of the room. She rushed forward to set another plate in front of Rey and Zander.

"Rey, this is Dyani," Seth said from across the table. "She's the sister of Ken. We got a van from him in Big Horn."

"My brother felt bad about the trade. He says your sword is worth much more than the old van he gave you," Dyani said with a wide smile as Zander studied the older woman. She had dark skin and jet-black hair streaked with gray. Wrinkles lined her face, but they appeared to be from smiling and not from hard years.

"Please, eat. You will be safe here. The government men will be hesitant to follow you unto my people's land," she said, and Zander saw a slight anger fill the woman's eyes.

"Ken was telling me his people once lived like the dragon warriors," Seth said quickly from across the table. "But the big government came and destroyed their way of living years ago. To compensate for the horrendous acts done upon them, they were given land."

"It's called a reservation," Dyani said from across the room as she served more food. "But my people still keep up with tradition."

"Why won't the government come here?" Rey asked as she started to eat.

"I called the tribe and they shut the road into town after you arrived," the woman explained with a smile. "The only other road in is far to the north."

"We have at least eight hours. Even if they bring their flying machines, Dyani said in the dark there are no landing places near here," Seth replied as he ate a large forkful of white roots.

"Tell me, how did you escape, and how did we all get here?" Rey demanded, and her dark eyes turned to Zander.

"I'm afraid your anger should be directed at me," Belent

said from the other side of the table. "The plan was mostly mine."

"Yes, but I agreed to it," Mateo said from the other table.

"Once we had you stored inside the truck, Mateo kept behind the wheel so we wouldn't lose you. The next step was locating Zander. I had seen the general's men take you into the center tent but couldn't get past the guards posted there. Even after Corbin's distraction," Belent said as he pushed the plate away and sat back in his chair.

"The shooting didn't distract the general, and they had cameras on me, so my illusional magic wouldn't work inside the tent," Zander explained with a shake of his head.

"The plan required you outside, not in the tent," Belent said with a nod. "But to do that we needed them to lead you out."

"I figured the shooting was my rescue," Zander stated. He turned to smile at Rey. "But I thought it was you." He grabbed a stray strand of her black hair and gave it a gentle tug.

"I would have, but I was tied up at the moment," she said. After a moment, she stood and reached inside her pocket. When Zander saw her pull his mother's swan bracelet from her pocket, he frowned in confusion.

"How did you get that?" It was Belent who had spoken Zander's own question. The sorcerer leaned forward and studied the small object in question.

"It was my birthday present from Princess Charlotte," Rey exclaimed as she sat back down and held the bracelet out for them to see. "I still had the package, but when I opened it..."

"Let me guess, your bonds fell off," Zander said with a smile.

"Well, yes," Rey said with confusion.

"Then it is yours." Zander reached forward and tied the bracelet's leather strap around her left wrist.

"My gift served you as well as it did the queen," Belent said with a shake of his head. "It's magical and frees the wearer of any bonds."

"Yours?" Rey asked and studied the beautiful swan now resting on her wrist.

"An old gift from one who was unaware of his own magic. I think our Princess Charlotte knew you would have more need of it than our queen at the moment."

Zander saw worry cross Belent's face, and he too thought briefly of his parents.

"So," Rey said finally, drawing their attention back to their story. "How did you get Zander?"

"I knew I would need to get out of the tent," he supplied, giving her a wink. He set aside his worry for his family temporarily and turned back to the story. "So, I gave them what they wanted."

"What?" Rey asked, her eyes wide.

"I told them that the magic I held had been passed down from my mother and that only gods could wield it." Another wink was sent to Rey as she frowned at him. "I said I was a god and if they didn't release me that I would blow them away. When they didn't go for that, I told them I was an alien, and my ship was coming back to get me."

"That one almost caused you more trouble than you could handle," Belent stated with a shake of his head.

"I would have handled it," Zander stated, turning to his mentor. "Well, maybe."

"Luckily, I was just outside, listening. I knew Zander would be stuck in there forever if left on his own, so I used my magic and sent bats to attack the general's men," Belent stated.

"Something my mother wouldn't have liked, due to her trip down into the Kylix," Zander said with a shake of his head.

"It was her fear of them that gave me the idea," Belent said with a smile.

"Once the tent was full of the small creatures, they had to open the flaps, and I was able to get in and release Zander from his bonds," Belent supplied with a wave of his hand. "Then we went to the truck and waited."

"Waited?" Rey asked, confusion written on her face.

"Well, if we had raced out of there, they would have chased us. We had Corbin and Mateo already in position, so when the general's men 'gave chase,' they had no clue we were in on the chase," Belent said with a smile.

"We were one of the last trucks to drive out of the compound," Corbin said with a smile. "Took up the rear, so to speak."

"Once the general's men reached a branch in the road, we took the one back to where the others were. After confirming our destination, we immediately started this way," Belent supplied.

"And where were you?" Rey asked, turning to study Zander.

"I was hiding in the box next to you, out of sight but just a bit cramped," he said with a grimace. His right knee still ached from a rather hard hit against the side of his own box.

"The good news is, we are less than a day away from our destination now," Seth said with a smile.

"As long as we don't run into any more trouble," Avaline said from beside Corbin.

"But won't the general be waiting for us? How was he able to get to us, by the way?" Rey asked with concern in her voice.

"I think the cameras at the gas station gave us away, remember?" Zander continued only after she had finally nodded. "They must have seen the van in one of those."

"But what's to stop them from finding us again?" Rey asked.

"You will be driving a different van now," Dyani said as she started to clean the table. Avaline and Kenzo quickly jumped up to aid with the clean-up while the others started moving the table and chairs back. Before long the room was cleaned, and Zander followed the little woman outside to study their new means of transportation while Rey was given clean clothes and pointed in the direction of a hot shower.

The van was large. It had four rows of long seats in the back and dark tinted windows to block out the sun's heat and prying eyes. There was a painting of a deer on both sides of the dark van along with a logo of the Running Deer Casino.

"This will get you north where you need to go," Dyani said as she handed Zander a set of keys.

"We need to pay you," he stated, but Dyani shook her head. "Please, it is the way of our people." He reached down and removed his boot knife, which he had gotten back from Corbin, and showed it to her. "This is Feirn. It means sting in the dragon warrior tongue."

The woman's dark eyes went wide as he held the small blade out for her to inspect.

"The blade is strong, and the handle is made from the tusk of the great horned fish."

"It's beautiful," Dyani whispered as she took the knife. "It's so light!" she quickly exclaimed.

"The Draydon tribe's blacksmith uses only the strongest materials," he said with a smile.

"I thank you, but I fear that this blade is more valuable than the van." She bowed her head.

"No, you give us a chance to return home. That is what we value beyond anything," Zander replied with a smile.

13

ONE TO TEN

They left Dyani's home early the next morning while it was still dark. They didn't want to place her or her people in any more danger than they had already, so they only remained one short night.

Zander drove the new van as Corbin sat in the passenger seat and gave him directions according to the map Dyani had drawn up for them.

"Stay off the main freeways," she had told them before they left. "Take the side roads. Most are near the rivers, and there are no easy places for a big government convoy to travel."

"We cannot thank you enough," Rey told the woman as she embraced Dyani in a fierce hug. "Our tribe thanks yours."

The map had them taking a small dirt road north from the town by means of the mountains. When they passed the roadblock of large dirty trucks with large dark-skinned and black-haired men standing around, Zander gave them a wave and was quietly thankful the men were friends of Dyani and not their enemy.

They didn't pass many towns after that. The road wound gently along a steep valley. They saw neither road signs nor homes, and he had the feeling they were in a wide empty area, which made him think of the Highman Plains in Genoa.

When the road started heading west, the sun was just starting to peek up from behind them. They had crossed a small river and finally farmlands could be seen as the valley opened up for a time.

After they had traveled for several more miles, they moved into a vast expanse of open plains. For miles, all they could see were tall grasses waving in the wind on both sides of the empty road.

When they stopped for gas in a little town that consisted of only four buildings, Zander changed places with Corbin. They weren't worried about video cameras here as the gas station was small and the building was very old. The young man behind the counter couldn't even grow facial hair and didn't give the large van a second glance. Belent paid using the credit card.

When he returned to the van, Zander sat in one of the seats in back and closed his eyes to rest for a while and let Corbin drive. The previous day's activities and full night of capture and escape had finally caught up to him.

When he woke a few hours later, the signs let him know they were just outside a town called Great Falls. Rubbing his eyes, he turned to see Rey studying him from the seat directly behind him.

"How did you sleep?" she asked, her dark eyes scanning him. He saw a worry line form between her brows.

He tried to stretch his long legs in the confined space and then rubbed his sore neck as she continued to watch him.

"I slept. But I feel like I was shoved in a box for several hours then slept on a rock for several more," he replied. Her soft laugh at his comments made up for some of his discomfort.

"Here, let me help." She leaned forward and ran her hands along his neck. "You have a huge knot here," she said when her strong fingers found the sore spot.

"I must have—ow!" He leaned away from her hands as she hit a tender spot on the back of his head.

"Oh, don't be such a baby." She grabbed his shoulders then pulled him back to lean against the chair again. By the time she had worked out the worst of his aches, they had reached the outskirts of Great Falls.

"Dyani was worried about the base here," Belent said from the front seat. "She said it was an air base for the military."

"I think she said we couldn't get around it without adding several hours to our trip," Corbin stated as he maneuvered the van towards the town.

"Look," Kenzo said from the front row of seats. "What is that?"

They all looked and saw a small fence on the right side of the road. A little white building stood behind it and a vast field lay beyond. Neither of these things should cause alarm, but behind the small building, Zander saw what had worried his friend.

Two black air ships hovered along the edge of the road as a massive airplane took off from the ground. The ship's movement caused hot air to curl behind it as it rose above the very road the van was traveling along.

"Cats!" hollered Rey as they all ducked, as if the plane would chop their heads off from inside the van. The roar of the machine was deafening, and Zander fought the urge to cover his ears from the noise.

"Have they found us?" Corbin asked as he tried to keep the van on the road.

"I do not think so," Belent said as he studied the scene. "They do not give chase."

"Maybe we should turn around?" Corbin quickly asked.

"No, that will draw attention to us," Zander said. He wished he were the one driving. "But we have to assume there will be a military presence in this town."

"That's what I would have done if I were leading the chase. I would try and cut off any escape route. Try and block my quarry's pathways if I knew where they were going." Rey said with a shake of her head.

"So, what do we do?" Corbin asked quickly.

"Let me see the map," Zander said. Belent quickly handed it back and then came to sit next to him.

"Hm. There are several ways out of town," Zander stated as he studied the lines on the paper.

"Three major roads," Belent confirmed. Rey moved over so she could see the map better.

"What's this one?" She pointed at a blue line.

"Water. That's the river," Zander said with a shake of his head.

"If we can get across the river, we can take this little road, see this one that goes along the fields." Belent pointed to a faint little line. "See how it follows the fields. Then it heads right back to the main road on the other side of town."

"If we can get across the river." Zander quickly moved to sit next to Corbin and directed him to take the next right.

There were only four bridges besides the main one in town, according to the map, and Zander was concerned all of them would be blocked. If they were in Genoa, that's where he would have set up blockades.

But things seemed to work differently here than they did in Genoa. Maybe the government here couldn't block major roads without a good reason. And since General Wilberg and his men were on a manhunt for "aliens," he imagined their hunt was secretive. Hopefully that would work in their favor.

The first bridge they took was clear of any blockades, and they all breathed a huge sigh of relief. Corbin turned the van westward again. They had just hit the main road when traffic backed up.

"This doesn't look good," Corbin said as he studied the cars ahead.

"I see flashing lights," Zander said and quickly studied the map. "Turn here," he directed and soon the van was bumping along a small dirt road. "Belent, can you turn the van invisible?"

"Yes," Belent replied from the back as Zander twisted in his seat to study the road they had just left. "Look, they are having all the cars turn off into that field."

"The blockade," Rey hissed. "Can we get around?'

"I don't know. The map shows this goes back east. Let me look," Zander said as Rey moved forward to help him study the map.

"There's a way, but it's all small roads." She traced the path with her finger. "See, we will end up going way east then north before getting back onto the right road."

"Eventually the river will block us, but these small roads will get us many miles away from this blockade," Zander exclaimed. He had Corbin take the next right.

They drove through farmland for several miles. Breakfast was long overdue and all of them were tired of getting thrown around from the van hitting bumps on the pitted dirt roads. Before they hit the main road again, tempers were high.

Upon reaching the main road, they came across a small rest area. They all had a quick trip to the bathroom and used a food machine to obtain a small breakfast.

Zander had five candy bars and two small bags of chips, then washed it all down with two tubes of something called Coke. After this pit stop, he drove again and found his mind wandered excessively while his foot tapped uncontrollably.

"We will want to avoid every major town," Rey said from the passenger seat next to him. "I have used the pencil and drawn the way I think we should take to avoid each town."

He nodded and continued to tap his foot.

"Are you listening?" she asked as he turned to study her.

"Yeah, just twitchy."

"We need to find better food," she mumbled. She crossed her arms as a scowl covered her pretty face.

The next town was easy to avoid as the river was smaller and there were several side roads both in farm fields and along the river's shallow valley. But Rey voiced her worry over the larger town called Shelby that they were fast approaching.

"If we turn off well before the town, we will need to go out of our way. We could turn before the river and head over here. There are towns, but they are considerably smaller than this big one."

She continued to mumble to herself until Zander demanded to know which road to take.

"Here, turn here. We will avoid the main roads."

He saw her bite the nail on her right thumb, a sure sign she was nervous about her decision.

They drove into the next small town and stopped to fill the van up with gas and to get some supplies. The heat of the day was fading as the sun started its descent in the west.

Rey smelled the water, dust, and cooking food. As Corbin started to fill the van with gas, she made her way into the small but tidy convenience store.

She was thankful there was real food and stopped Zander from getting any more of the Coke drink, as she felt it made him too wired. He pouted a little and settled for a Powerade. She had worried about the name of the drink until she read on the label it was a sports drink.

The town itself was small, only a few blocks long, and their appearance didn't seem too unusual, as there were several work vans and trucks in the same gas station they pulled into.

After this stop, they all piled in again, and the van turned north once more. Fields of green grass and odd plants lined the small road for a while as they zigged and zagged north. When they came to another river surrounded by odd black hills, Rey marveled at their color.

"I wonder what makes the soil so dark," she said as they crossed the bridge.

"Who cares," Corbin said from behind them.

It took several more hours of navigating small roads and one little two-lane freeway for them to get back on the path Dyani had outlined for them.

"The hardest part will be this border," Rey said,

chewing her thumbnail again. "Dyani said we need papers to cross."

"I will take care of that," Belent said from the back of the van.

"I hope that once we are in another country, the general will not be able to follow," Zander said as he drove.

"You don't think he will be able to follow?" she asked, studying his profile.

"I don't know. It might be better if we wait until dark," Zander replied thoughtfully.

They traveled in silence for a while, and Rey kept moving her eyes between the road, the map, and Zander. Snores and muffled talking kept floating forward from the back of the van, and the smell of their last meal hung thick in the van's interior.

"Rey, I've been thinking," Zander finally said, his voice low.

"Yes?" she asked as more perfectly lined up rows of plants passed outside the windows.

"If we are captured again," he said, and she quickly shook her head.

"We are ahead of them now," she said, but the fear of another capture still filled her.

"*If*," he said and turned to look at her. "If we are, I might have another idea."

"Idea?" she asked, her mind blank to his intentions as she continued to study the map.

"My dad can do it. I mean, he's been trying to coach me on how to do it, but up till now, I haven't really tried hard," Zander mumbled.

Hearing Zander stumble over his own words brought her attention away from the map. She turned partially in the chair to study him and saw his face flushed. His large hands gripped the steering wheel hard, which indicated his discomfort at the direction of their conversation.

"I don't think I ever really tried hard because, well, Corbin teased me once about turning into a big fluffy Sniffer."

"What in the king's name are you talking about?" she asked as the tips of Zander's ears turned red.

"The royal gift," he replied.

Her eyes grew wide with this statement, and she leaned closer to him in eager anticipation. "Yes?"

"Well, I mean, you know of my illusions." He watched as she nodded her head for him to continue, then turned his eyes quickly back to the road. "Well, Dad has another... how shall I say it?" He paused and she counted the seconds until he formulated the right words. "Another gift. He can appear as a Beowulf."

"Really?" she exclaimed, and Zander quickly shushed her.

"Not everyone needs to know this," he whispered.

"So, you..." she asked, and he turned his eyes towards her with a shake of his head. The thought of him transforming into a creature both excited and awed her.

"I haven't found my form yet," he replied.

"You can choose?" She realized her little knowledge of royal magic hadn't taught her anything about this type of gift.

"Yes. At least Dad said he could," Zander explained, and Rey heard frustration fill his voice. "Belent has been trying to instruct me on using this gift, but I've just been too busy. No, that's not true, I've been too lazy."

She placed her hand on his on the wheel and gave it a gentle sympathetic squeeze.

"Your schedule has been busy since coming of age, and

it probably didn't help having to do drills with me," she said with a smirk.

"I know you're teasing me." He twisted his hand until he was holding hers. "Anyway, I think I have an idea for the form I want to use. But I wanted to run my thoughts by you first."

"Me?" she asked in confusion. "Why me?"

"Rey, don't you know?" He once again glanced her way. His sharp green eyes studied hers, and she felt herself getting lost in their depths.

"Uh," she managed before he smiled at her and winked then turned his eyes back to the road.

"You have great tactical skills," he finally replied with a grin.

When she tried to yank her hand from his, he laughed and held on tighter.

"Just kidding. You know why, don't you?" he said, his voice more sober this time.

His last statement was more a whisper than a question, and she felt her face heat with emotions as her heart beat a little faster. Yes, she knew why. At least she thought she did.

"Zander—" she started, but then Corbin stuck his head between them.

"Hey, what's the plan?" Corbin asked.

"My lad," Zander said as he continued to drive with his left hand on the wheel and his right still hold Rey's. "What do you know about the lore of dragons here on this planet?"

14

THE FLIGHT OF THE PRINCE

The last town that lay before the border between the United States and the country to its north was quite large. It was too large for Zander's liking, but Belent thought it was wiser to stop in a busy city. They went to a popular eatery to enjoy a midday meal, breaking into small groups. Belent ensured no electronics would record them while Zander adjusted their images.

Rey, Corbin, Belent, and he all sat at one table. They quietly talked about their plans while the others milled about and ate their meals.

"We should wait until night," Rey urged, mirroring Zander's own thoughts.

"Time is running out. If we wait, that may give them more time to catch us or set another trap," Corbin insisted, and Zander saw Belent nod in agreement.

"The border will be our most dangerous passing. If we allow them time to gather and block it, then we might be stuck in this country, and this world."

"How much farther is it?" Zander asked. Rey pulled the map out and leaned over it.

"Less than an hour away," she finally provided.

"Waiting will cost us a whole day," Corbin insisted.

"Should we split up again?" Rey asked. Her eyes traveled to where their friends sat, all scattered about the restaurant.

"It might be wise," Belent stated, shaking his dark head.

"I don't think it will be needed," Zander advised, and his eyes turned to Rey's. "I might have a plan."

His plan took time, but he thought it was well organized. In the end, they found three families who were also there in the border town, heading in the same direction. These families were also in the restaurant getting lunch before heading home to Canada. With Rey's help, Zander befriended them and talked about their 'vacation' up north.

The Franks were a family of four who had traveled down to a place called Yellowstone on their school break trip. Their oldest child, Sarah, was a sour-looking girl with bright pink hair and a nose ring. The girl perked up a bit when Zander smiled her way. The youngest was a boy about ten named Brad. He studied Zander with open admiration when he told the family he had never been outside the good US of A.

"Really?" Brad asked with a shake of his blonde head. "Not even to Hawaii?"

"He's fascinated with the islands," the mother replied. Her soft brown eyes kept studying Zander.

"Nope, never been." Zander smiled as he drew Rey closer to his side. "Me and the missus have done lots of road trips, but this will be our first trip north," he said with a wink.

He saw Corbin and Avaline nod their heads in his direction as they chatted up another family. Zander listened to the Franks as he swept his eyes around the restaurant. Mika and Leon had approached another couple with no children and, after a minute, gave him the signal that they too had made contact with a family heading to the border.

Zander's plan had been simple. Gather as many earthlings as possible who were heading to Canada and try to synchronize their journey. If there was a roadblock, the more witnesses, the better. At least for what he had in mind.

"Are you in that big van?" Mr. Frank's question interrupted Zander's thoughts.

"What?" Zander followed the man's pointed finger and saw the native tribe's van. "Oh, why?" he asked, not wanting to answer the question, in case he needed to add a false image over the vehicle before they reached the border.

"Well, I know the native casino vehicles usually aren't allowed over the border," Mr. Frank said with a frown. "We don't get many of the southern tribes up north, if you know what I mean."

Zander didn't know, but he nodded his head quickly. "No, my car's around back."

"Ah, we have the newest wagon. It does better on the ice that we get up north." Mr. Frank then proceeded to talk about the make of their car.

Their trip was delayed by only two hours, then the band from Genoa shuffled quickly and quietly back into the casino van. Zander quickly adjusted its appearance to a large black SUV. All twelve from Geno still fit in the van, and Corbin started driving out of the parking lot.

They spotted the Franks, the Millers, and the Bradmans, a young newly married couple heading home after their honeymoon. They had waited in the parking lot so their departure would mirror the others. They followed the three cars out of town and unto the road heading north.

There were commercial trucks and other cars on the road as well.

Corbin matched his speed with the other cars as the miles passed slowly. Each step that they drew closer to the border, Zander grew more nervous.

"Relax," Rey said from behind him. "It's a good plan." She patted him on his shoulder.

"Just concentrate," Belent insisted.

"The map shows the Canadian inspection is after the border. The Franks said that is where they will search us," Rey supplied.

"If we get that far," Zander mumbled.

The sun was inching its way to their left when they passed the last intersection, and they finally spotted the first of the border buildings in the distance.

"Well, here we go," Corbin said, and Zander could tell his friend was having fun, no doubt thinking this whole trip was another grand escapade.

"Just stick to the plan," Zander warned. Corbin's grin widened.

They didn't even make it to the first building before trouble was upon them. A good hundred yards before the border, they saw the first of General Wilberg's men.

Ugly green trucks blocked the entire roadway forward, and they watched with concern as first the Miller's car and then the Frank's was stopped. When Zander saw the men open the car doors and drag the children out, he became enraged.

"What are they doing?" Rey hissed.

"No doubt searching for us," Belent replied, and Zander watched the sorcerer quickly disappear to protect Ben from being discovered. Belent had been concerned that his image would be used against the other Belent, or Ben. He had insisted that, at whatever costs, his current image must be hidden from the general and all video imagery. Luckily, they had all agreed to this and even luckier had been the solution. The sorcerer must remain invisible during all contacts with the general.

"Okay, phase one," Zander said, closing his eyes in concentration.

Zander's magical image of a black SUV shimmered and quickly turned into a large tank. Zander had seen one in the movies and had been fascinated by the machines. Large metal treads beat down the road as the image of its massive gun pointed right at the army trucks.

"I'm swinging left," Corbin shouted at him, and he adjusted the image as they drew close to the roadblock. "There's two of them, but the others have imaging visors on." This is what Zander was worried about. He had learned while captured in the camp that these visors blocked out his illusional magic.

The general knew of his illusions and even in the last camp had used video imaging to keep him from using his magic. But they had something the general didn't know about. They had Belent.

"Okay, aiming right. See that single car blocking the road on the right?" Zander asked and, in his mind, had the tank's gun taking aim.

"I've got it," Belent said as he stuck his right arm out of the van's open side window.

"Now!" Zander screamed and, for the first time, he and Belent combined their magic to flash his image and the sorcerer's blasting magic at the vehicle. The following explosion reminded Zander of the movies he and Corbin had enjoyed several nights ago.

"Yes," Rey screamed and pointed to the now mobile

military. "They are scrambling. But there are too many and they are still blocking the way."

"Not for long." Zander quickly gave new instructions to Belent.

They had wanted to give the men a warning before firing on them. After all, they didn't want to kill anyone. Just escape. Zander's warning shot had done what it was meant to. Most of the men ran from their vehicles, which still sat blocking the road. As he pointed the tank's gun at them, the men fled.

"Ready for the second shot?" He pointed at the truck he had the tank's gun aimed at.

"Ready," Belent said as he pointed his magic in that direction.

Another big explosion rocked the van, and Zander realized they were too close this time. Some of the fire singed the paint and the heat could be felt inside the van.

"We can't hit any more without hitting ourselves," he said, and called for phase two.

The tank's image shuffled and morphed into a large bulldozer. Belent used his magic to push the trucks and cars that were blocking their path off the road. They knew of the cement roadblocks, and Corbin swerved to avoid the permanent structures while magic was used on the others.

"The families are safe inside the structure," Rey announced, and Zander felt her hand tighten on his shoulder. "Any minute now," she warned as the first shot was fired by the military.

"I have the bubble up," Belent stated as their van barreled down the road towards the border. Several more trucks came at them, all blocking their path to freedom and home.

"I'm trying," Zander said as the blockage loomed ahead of them.

Trying to keep the illusion up was costing him. Much like his mother, he had to replenish when he used large quantities of his magic. He focused on his plan and not the nagging drop in energy.

"Ready," he stated as he turned off his illusional magic and felt himself slip deep down inside himself.

"Phase three," he heard Rey shout as the world around him dropped away.

The dragon appeared out of nowhere next to their van.

Large green scales glimmered in the afternoon light as leathery wings beat the air in its flight. To Rey, the dragon didn't seem unusual. In fact, it reminded her very much of home, which caused her to smile. Its long body was tucked under the thin but massive wings as it lifted up and away from their position.

She noticed that the dragon's green eyes were the same green as Zander's eyes. Its sharp claws flexed once as the wings sought warmer air. Zander, as the dragon, swung his head towards the encroaching army ahead, and she laughed at the excitement in his eyes.

"Go get them," she hissed in Zander's ear next to her.

Zander's body was still inside the van. He was deep in a trance while his royal magic allowed him to be in an alternative form outside. The dragon form he had chosen was one of great design and mirrored the dragons found along the

Cliffs of Faro. He had only altered it in one way from the dragons found in Genoa. This one breathed fire.

Rey's smile widened as the dragon drew close to the men along the road. She saw those who wore the video headgear go running and screaming away, their hands covering their heads as they shouted at those near them.

"It's real," they shouted at their fellow soldiers.

"You bet your ass it's real," Corbin shouted as he continued to plow down the road.

Belent's magic pushed the cars and trucks out of their way while he himself remained invisible.

"Look at his fire." Corbin's shout interrupted Rey's inspections of the remaining blockade.

"It's green," Seth said from behind her, and she turned in time to see the dragon swoop down and blow a big stream of green flames at an empty truck that sat yards away from the Canadian border patrol building.

"Cats," she whispered, and smiled. Dragons in Genoa didn't have the capability to breathe fire, so this was new and a bit exciting to her.

"Get that last one and we are clear," Corbin said as he swerved the van towards the now-open road.

"Look, it's the general," Mateo said from the back of the van.

Turning quickly, Rey saw the man standing in the middle of the road. He held a gun up and was firing at the van's tires to no avail.

"Did he get them all?" Corbin asked from the driver's seat.

"He's going back for two more flying vehicles. Then he should be done," Seth stated. They all watched as Zander's dragon swooped down two more times, his green flames engulfing a patrol car and a helicopter.

The general turned his gun towards the dragon, and Rey screamed. Fear engulfed her as the dragon dropped quickly to the ground.

"Zander," she cried. She turned forward and saw his body jolt once before his eyes flew open in shock.

"I'm fine," he whispered, but Rey saw that his forehead was damp, and his skin was very pale.

"Food, here, eat." She shoved a bar into his hands. He was shaking too much to rip the package open, so she quickly grabbed the Snickers, tore the package, and held it to his mouth.

"Next time, let's not do that on an empty stomach," she insisted, and he nodded weakly.

"Only one car behind us," Corbin said as Belent turned and pointed his fingers out the window. "Scratch that. We're clear," Corbin stated after the sorcerer sent a blast of magic at the pursuing car's tires.

It took Zander some time to recover. Rey was glad when he closed his eyes and finally fell asleep. His color was still off, but she hoped that the four candy bars and two power drinks would help him recover quickly.

The general's helicopter had been destroyed in the battle along the border, but still Rey kept an eye open for any signs of pursuit. She feared that the first city they hit would be barricaded and they would once again find themselves in a battle.

They all agreed to bypass the small town by using the farm streets. Dirt roads zigged and zagged around the major roads, which allowed for safe passage, though they grew tired of being jarred by the bumps.

Despite their quick speed, it seemed to take forever for them to make their way northwest. More small towns and dirt roads led finally into the mountains.

At the first sight of the hills, she felt a great sense of relief. They weren't as tall as the ones outside the vast city of Denver. No snow lingered here on the peaks, but they were still impressive.

They traveled through several smaller cities nestled inside the mountains, cities that were narrow and long, with hundreds of small homes. Little inns and stores lined the road, which twisted and turned in the wide valley. When the road wound between a vast lake and several massive mountains, Zander finally opened his eyes.

"Here, do you need more food?" she asked as she felt his forehead to check if he had a temperature.

"I'm fine. Just feel empty, is all." He pushed her hand away. "Got any of those chips?"

"Here ya go." Seth handed him a large bag of the potato chips.

"There is another drink here too." Rey smiled as he ate a whole handful of chips. "They want to start calling you dragon breath," she informed him with a smile.

"I thought hot head was better," Seth interjected, and Zander groaned.

"I'll never live this down," he mumbled.

"Just don't do that near the Drakaina and you'll be fine," Rey advised, speaking of the female dragons that roosted on the cliffs along the ocean.

"I don't know if I can ever do that again," Zander replied. He turned his green eyes towards her. "But it was a kick in the butt to be able to fly."

The road moved down out of the high mountains and into a valley. Tall dark green trees lined the road on either side as the road continued to twist and turn downwards. When they finally came to fields and small homes, Rey told them they were close.

"There." She pointed out the right side of the van. "See that mountain? It's called the Three Sisters. The falls is at the bottom."

"Where is Ben?" Zander asked. He turned his head to look at Belent.

"He owns a hotel up in the mountains there. The Twisted Pines," Belent advised. He moved to study the map that Rey still held. "There."

"But nothing's there." She drew the paper closer for another inspection.

"No, but it is there," Belent said with a smile. "I can feel it."

"Do you think we lost the general?" Zander asked from the front seat.

"No, but I do not think we will have much more time here on Earth to fear him," Belent said grimly. "Here, turn up this road," he advised Corbin, who took the right turn a bit too fast.

The mountains loomed ahead. Rey saw the tall peaks covered with dark green pines. Three jagged peaks speared up ahead; their rocky tops seemed to point straight upwards, as if in defiance of the other mountains around them. In their shadows she noticed small islands of snow dotted near their base. When trees blocked her vision of the mountains, she returned her gaze to the map.

"There, see that sign?" Belent pointed to a large wooden sign.

"Twisted Pines Inn," Corbin read as he turned the car up the paved road. "Wow, it looks big."

The sign had a picture on it as well, a vast structure shaped in the wood and outlined in gold paint. It was six stories tall and sat in front of the Three Sisters mountains.

The road led them upwards, with trees on either side of

the road. There were several homes along the road, and the structures grew larger in size and further apart the higher they climbed. Soon there were metal gates lining the road and the homes were replaced with a thick forest.

At one point they came out onto a cliff face, and Corbin stopped the car suddenly. A quarter of a mile from their stopping point sat the majestic inn. Rey thought this was where the picture from the sign must have been taken. The Three Sisters peaks loomed into the sky. They were each impressive on their own, but together they were extraordinary.

But it was the vast inn at the mountains' base that took her breath away.

"It reminds me of home," Zander said with a smile, and she suddenly realized that the Twisted Pines Inn was a smaller version of Castle Pines. Instead of being built with vast Genoa stone slabs, this building was made of wood and smaller square red stones.

The main building had square sides that flanked an impressive, curved center. Sparkling windows lined the front, and several chimneys could be seen pointing into the afternoon sky.

Several smaller buildings sat surrounding the impressive structure, each painted a bright color with a bright red or brown roof. Glass shone in the late afternoon light, and they could see the movement of cars and several hundred people.

An odd movement caught her eye as it ran up the vast mountain to one side of the town. She focused on this and saw little square cars gliding upwards, as if magic guided them. They traveled between vast poles and headed up to the top of hill.

"There must be over a hundred rooms," Corbin said as he leaned forward to get a better look at the inn.

"And Belent—I mean, Ben—is here?" Rey asked. She turned to study Belent.

"Let's find out," Corbin answered, and he started the van again.

15

THE TWISTED PINES

Zander's eyes grew wide as his friend drove the van towards the massive building.

Shops and businesses lined the roads of the village, and people milled about, either eating or shopping. The smell of food drifted in, which made his stomach growl. He smelled meats, sweets, and a hint of ale, which made him smile.

The twisted road led them up the valley and finally around to the right of the Twisted Pines itself. Corbin pulled into a four-level parking area that had signs stating parking was free for those staying at the inn. The parking structure descended lower than the main floor of the inn.

"Park here, we will scope it out first," Rey insisted.

"Not all of us," Zander insisted and turned to Belent. "Maybe you should stay?"

"No, I will go, but I will be invisible. Just in case." With no further delay, the sorcerer disappeared as he sat inside the van.

"I can't get used to him doing that," Corbin said with a shake of his head.

"I am invisible, not deaf," came Belent's frustrated voice.

"Right. I forget that too," Corbin mumbled next to Zander, who smiled and opened his door.

"Corbin and I, along with Belent, will check things out," Zander said.

Rey grabbed his arm firmly.

"And Rey," he finally added with a sigh.

They walked up two flights of stone steps to the entrance of the inn.

"Well, let's see if you're home," Zander finally said.

Wooden tables with bright red umbrellas and chairs sat along the wide stone landing and at each were men and women enjoying their evening meal. The smells of cooked meat and rich spices drifted his way, causing his stomach to grumble yet again.

"You just ate," Rey reminded him as he smiled.

"Yeah, but being a dragon takes a lot out of a man." He drew her closer to his side.

"I didn't eat, and I'm starving, if it's any concern to you," Corbin added, but he followed them as they moved towards the inn's double-wide glass doors.

The doors led into a high-ceilinged room painted a bright gold. Dark wood trimmed the walls and surrounded a stone fireplace that took up one full wall. Soft couches and seats surrounded the hearth. More people milled about here.

Along the left side of the room sat a long wooden desk. Three people worked this station. Two were women, one a tiny young redhead and the other an older white-haired woman, while the third was an elderly bald black man.

"Welcome to Twisted Pines," the redhead said with a

smile as they approached. "My name's Franny. How may I help you?"

"Um," Zander said, and his mind went blank. Should he ask for Ben? Should he state they were the owner's friends? What if he wasn't here? What if it wasn't Belent or a future/past version of Belent who came out?

"We need several rooms," Rey interjected as she stepped forward.

"Yes, we can help with that. How many will you require?" Franny asked politely as she looked down at the computer screen near her.

"Franny," came a familiar voice. To Zander's shock and relief, he saw Belent walk out of a door behind the counter. "I believe this is the group I was awaiting."

"Be..." Corbin said but was interrupted when the man's eyes turned and squinted in warning at him. "Ben," Corbin quickly adjusted his original statement and stepped back with a nod of his head.

This Belent, or Ben, was nearly identical to their friend, but there were some small differences. Ben had short hair and no sideburns. He was dressed in a fine black suit with a bright red tie. The eyes were still intense, but Zander noticed a few more lines around their edges. His smile was genuine. A single gold ring flashed on his right pinky.

"Ah, the Genoa Foundation," Franny said with a smile. "Yes, we have your rooms prepared for you. I believe ten rooms total on the top floor, east wing." She clicked a few buttons on her computer, and a machine behind her started to whirl.

"I can show them to their rooms," Ben said as Franny nodded.

"Yes, Mr. Boon," Franny replied with another smile. She handed the man several cards. "These are your keys," she told Zander. "They will get you into the rooms along with the conference room at the end of the west wing, first floor."

"Once they are settled, I will give them a tour myself." Ben smiled at the woman. "Thanks, Franny."

"You're welcome, sir." She turned back and smiled at them. "Enjoy your stay."

"Here, we will take the elevator. Then once in the room, we can talk freely." Ben ushered them down to the end of the room and past a wide set of wooden stairs leading upwards.

When he stopped outside a set of small doors and pushed a round button next to him, they all stared at him in confusion.

"Elevators," he explained. "They are faster."

Still confused by his statement, Zander watched as the two doors opened, revealing a very small room beyond.

"Please, go ahead and enter," Ben urged. Once in, he pushed a button that had a 6 on it and turned to smile at them as the room started to move. "You turn to face the doors," he explained. Zander and Rey turned around.

"Are you?" Rey started to ask but stopped when Ben held up his hand to silence her.

"Not yet." He looked around at their faces. "But might I say, it is good to see you again."

The room they were in—the elevator, as Ben called it—stopped moving and the doors once again opened. This time, instead of the lobby of the inn, they were facing a wide hallway with an alcove full of chairs.

"Here we are." Ben ushered them out and to their left. The hall was long and wide and moved off in both directions.

They reached the first room, and Ben used the odd square key to enter.

The room was huge. There were high, white ceilings, and the room was filled with soft golden colors. There were two queen beds along one wall and a door to a white bathroom on another. Beyond that door sat a large sofa and armchair.

There was a balcony with a view of the high cliffs, and Zander noted a flash of water. Upon closer inspection, he realized that Fairy Falls must lay just outside the hotel.

Once they were all through the door, it was quickly shut, and Ben smiled wildly. "Okay, where are you?" he asked to the room. His smile widened as Belent reappeared next to Zander. "I knew it." He beamed and shook his head. "I knew you could do it."

"Of course, you did," Belent replied as Zander staired on in amazement.

There before them stood two identical men. One was a bit older and dressed in a very expensive suit while the other, their Belent, stood there in his borrowed clothing.

"The others are in the van still?" Ben asked. He didn't wait for an answer as he handed the room key to Corbin. "Corbin, be a lad and go fetch them. You can use the stairs at the end of the hall. Less attention that way."

After receiving a nod from their Belent, Corbin bowed once and headed for the door. Zander saw Rey move to the window to look out at the falls while he returned his attention to the two sorcerers.

"I have some questions," he stated. Both men turned to smile at him, which he found disconcerting.

"Of course, you do. I will be happy to answer any questions, but first, let's get you some food." Ben walked over to the phone sitting next to the first bed. "Yes, Carrie, please have Mr. Templeton bring the food to my private dining room and send for Ms. Stratton." After he placed the phone back on its receiver, he turned to smile at them again. "We will wait for the others, then head down to the rooms on the west side of this floor."

"Food?" Zander asked weakly and once again his stomach grumbled.

"Yes, I ordered enough for an army. An army from Genoa," Ben said with a smile.

The private dining room was a cozy room with one big table. The long table was set in the center and a crystal chandelier hung above, its light shining on white plates and golden utensils. Dark green napkins and a golden table-cloth made the table colorful. Bright white flowers were arranged in a low vase. A warm fire crackled in the stone fireplace on one wall, and wide windows looked out at the falls, which were over a hundred yards away from the building.

Rey's eyes widened as five servers came in, carrying the food on massive trays. She smiled when she smelled meat and spices and a pretty golden wine was poured into her glass. There was enough food to satisfy the hungry Genoa warriors, and maybe more.

"Welcome," Ben stated with a smile as a beautiful dark-haired woman walked into the room and stood next to him.

Rey thought the woman was about Ben's age. Her long dark hair had hints of gray around the temples and her brown eyes showed a few wrinkles, but her smile was genuine as she looked out at them.

"Friends, this is Shelly Stratton. She is my manager and dear friend." Ben grabbed the woman's hand and kept it in his. "She would be my wife if she would ever agree to it." Everyone looked shocked at this statement.

"I'm sure your friends don't want to hear about our relationship at the moment," Shelly stated but she stopped when the last server disappeared out the door.

"Please," Ben interrupted with a smile. "Shelly knows all about me. Belent, you can appear now, it is okay."

Shelly's eyes went wide with surprise as the younger Belent appeared feet from Ben and Shelly. Rey expected the woman to go pale or look confused, but she smiled.

"You look exactly like the day I met you," Shelly said. She turned to Ben. "So, the circle will close soon."

"Yes, my dear." Ben gently kissed Shelly's lips. "But first, let's eat. Afterwards, we will talk about the plans." He moved over to the table and raised his wine glass. "To Genoa and the queen."

All from Genoa stood and raised their own glasses. After the traditional salute was done, they all drank the fruity wine and then sat down to enjoy the meal.

"Now, my friends, enjoy." Ben assisted Shelly into a seat, then turned to where Zander and Rey sat on his left. "I already know your questions, so I will start at the beginning while you eat."

Zander nodded, and Rey turned to the small, cooked bird and pale white roots on her plate as she listened to Belent's tale.

"In my time—that is, Belent's current time—we were also successful in gaining the tomahawk from the museum. I believe the rip took place prior to your adventure at the museum," Ben started. He held up a hand as Zander tried to ask a question. "Yes, I know you don't understand, so I will try to explain. The rip. It is where two timelines or two possibilities merge. I felt it much like you did." Here he turned to Belent, who nodded once. "It was small and manifests itself in a way that only those with true deep magic can feel."

"Yes." Belent raised his glass and took a deep drink. "It hurt."

"I think I felt it too," Zander said to her surprise. "It was an intense headache while Rey and I were at the library."

"Yes," Ben said with a smile at Zander. "I knew you would." Here he turned and looked at Belent. "That was where your life and mine became separate. Therefore, I wasn't able to give you too much insight into what you would face here. Anyway, like you, I too obtained the tomahawk, but that was after a fierce battle with General Wilberg two towns prior. We had also escaped him in the large city of Denver. We lost Kylo there; a bullet ripped into his heart." Ben looked sad as his eyes landed on Kylo from across the room.

"What happened then?" Rey asked after a few moments of silence. She turned her eyes from Kylo's face and looked at Ben.

"Well, the tomahawk was ours, and we didn't see the army again until the border." Ben raised his glass and took a drink. "That's when the young prince here blasted them with his dragon. Tell me, what color was his fire?" he asked with a smile towards Zander.

"Green." Rey provided the answer with a smile.

The laughs that came from Belent and Ben were so alike it started another round of chuckles.

"How long did I try and teach you to choose your

form?" Ben asked with a shake of his head. "Oh well. Yes, the dragon was gold and green with green flames. I wasn't sure it would be similar, but it was a magnificent plan. Since your escape and mine were similar here, I can tell you a little of the results from the border attack. The TV news has been filled with a gas leak along the border. There were rumors of an attack, but the American government has tried to cover it up by shutting down the nearby town. The eyewitnesses have since changed their stories of alien attacks and seeing a large dragon. Their stories now match those the general's men have provided."

"But how did you get here?" Zander asked.

"When we arrived here, there was no hotel, no people around, only the wilderness and the waterfall. We were tired and hungry." Ben shook his head as his vision turned inward while he remembered. "I, not understanding the magic of this place, foolishly used the tomahawk on the falls, quite forcibly."

Rey saw the man's handshake as he reached for his glass of wine. After a slight hesitation, he reached over to hold Shelly's hand again.

"I was a fool," Ben continued. "I didn't understand that these falls are already part of Genoa."

"What?" Belent cried out, and Rey turned to study him. "So, the cut?"

"Yes. The cut is permanent," Ben provided with a shake of his head. "The chief's tomahawk sliced both the border in Earth and the one in Genoa itself." Turning, he studied Zander with sad eyes. "Let me explain. The Orick is a doorway. A door opens and closes based on the user. The Orick is a door that is always closed and can be opened when needed. What I did in my time, here at the falls, was break the door down."

"So, is it still open?" Belent's question had all eyes turning towards him.

"You, my friends, are sitting about a hundred yards from it right now," Ben said with a nod and a feeble smile. "The slashing of the barrier did send everyone home. But it cast the intruder, or me, out of my own world and time."

Ben quickly stood and turned to stand behind his chair, his long fingers wrapped around the wooden back as he looked down the table. Sorrow and regret were written on his face until he cast his eyes upon Shelly, then he smiled slightly.

Rey thought the man looked no more than ten years different from his counterpart. There was now gray hair sprinkled around his temples, and a few more lines around his eyes, but only small differences separated these two men.

"How long?" she asked, and Ben turned to smile at here.

"Not as long as you would think. I was sent sixty years back, Earth years. But for us, only fifteen seasons have passed."

"So long?" Rey asked and leaned forward.

"It hasn't been too bad," Ben said with a smile as his brown eyes turned to study Shelly once again. "I built my inn and have only had to fake my death once." He chuckled at their expressions and took his seat once again. "That is a story for another time." Ben waved his hands once again. "Let's just say I have gotten really good at aging myself." He waved a hand before his face and, to Rey's amazement, his face changed before her eyes. His hair grew white, his wrinkles increased, and he seemed to shrink down into the chair.

Sitting in the seat now was a man of over seventy years of age. He gave her a wink and waved his hand over his face again, quickly returning to his former appearance.

"The last time I did that was over forty Earth years ago. I, of course, left my generous estate to my son, Benjamin Boon the second." The smile he gave them was wide, and he sent another wink to Rey. "That is when I met Shelly and lost my heart."

"Despite my better judgment, so did I," Shelly said with a shake of her head and her own smile.

"I don't understand." Zander leaned towards them. "If we changed something, why are you still here then?"

"The rip is still here. That is why." Ben picked up the soft green tablecloth and studied it. Then he picked up the table knife. "See, here is the rip." With this he cut the cloth, leaving an inch long gash. "Nothing can or will close it. I could wash this, and the tear will remain. My people could sew it up, but still you would see where the rip had once been."

"So, despite us changing it, you must remain?" Belent asked.

"Yes. I have been charged to guard the tear. This is now my burden," Ben stated. His shoulders slumped again. "For all times."

16

THE INN

Zander fought off his exhaustion through the meal as he listened to Ben's explanation. There had been a few corrections from Shelly, but their story was incredible. The sorcerer seemed content and spoke of his time with humor and an ease that appeared to be missing in the Belent he knew. But long before dessert was rung for, Zander found his eyes heavy and his mind going numb.

"Yes, I agree. He looks beat." Ben's words startled Zander who turned and saw that Rey was standing beside his chair, her hand on his arm and a warm smile on her face.

"Up you go. Let's get you to your bed," she said with a shake of her head.

By the time she led him into his room, his head hurt, and he had to blink once or twice before he realized she was trying to take his shoes off.

"Here, let me help." He tried to help her but ended up sitting there watching her instead.

"It appears becoming a dragon is harder than your illusions," she said with a cluck of her tongue at him.

"I don't know how Dad does it," he mumbled. Rey

stopped to look at him. "Turning into a Beowulf," Zander explained and leaned back on the bed, still fully clothed. He placed his hands behind his head and stared up at the ornate ceiling and smiled. "First time my parents met; he was in wolf form."

"I never heard the story of how they met," she said, and he looked over to where she stood against the window, looking out at the falls. "He was in wolf form?" she asked with a laugh.

Zander didn't think he had the strength in him to laugh but found a chuckle emitting from his chest as he closed his eyes.

"Yes. It's a good thing he wasn't a dragon." With this, he drifted off into much needed sleep.

He dreamed of Caylee that night. Her long soft brown hair swirled in ringlets around her face as she stood surrounded by mist.

Concerned, Zander thought his twin had been enveloped in the red haze that had sent him and his friends to Earth. But when a smile slowly formed on Caylee's lips, he relaxed. He watched her for a minute then realized she didn't see him or know he was there.

"Caylee?" he said, but still she stood still. He tried again, but there was no response.

She was dressed in a lightweight blue cloak, the mist collecting on its collar and her face. When she tilted her head upwards, her hood dropped down along her back, and she gave a big sigh.

"You might catch a cold, Your Highness," came a deep rich voice, and Zander squinted his eyes as a dark figure materialized out of the mist behind his sister.

"Thank you, Captain Rouen." Caylee's tone had

Zander's eyes narrowing even more. Who was this captain? And why was his sister's voice almost breathless?

The dark shape took form, and Zander saw a tall man with jet-black hair appear. He had a tanned face with a night's growth of stubble on his chin. Full lips smiled at his sister as piercing tan eyes looked at her from under dark lashes.

Seeing how the man looked at his sister set Zander's teeth on edge. He flexed his hands as the captain approached his sister in the fog.

"We cannot have you catching a cold." The captain reached behind her and, after touching one of her dark locks, pulled her hood up and gently placed it on her head. "We should pass the Straight of Nereis tomorrow."

Caylee quickly looked over the captain's broad shoulders once, as if confirming they were alone, then said, "You said you saw Pescara before?"

The dark-haired captain nodded once, his eyes still intently focused on Caylee. He stood less than a foot from her. Zander saw that the man's hands were still holding his sister's hood.

"Did you, I mean, have you seen the tower of Della Val?" He had never heard his sister stumble over her words before and leaned forward to hear better.

"The blossom of Pescara is quite a vison to behold," Captain Rouen whispered. "The white tower shines in the day's light and its petal gently opens at the sun's apex." Again, the man's dark hand brushed his sister's hair, and Zander fought the urge to rush forward. "Beyond Pescara is unknown to many, but Enzo has traveled beyond its shores many times."

"Has he ever seen the Trillium?" Now Zander noticed that his sister was whispering.

"No." He lowered his head as if to kiss Caylee but stopped with his lips only inches from Caylee's. "No!" Captain Rouen growled, and Zander watched in shock as he twisted quickly and pulled a broad sword out of its sheath and aimed it right at Zander's heart.

Zander woke with the man's last scream still echoing in his head. He felt that the man's word wasn't a response to the question, but something deeper, something primal.

Zander unclenched his hands and realized his jaw was also clenched. He wiggled it back and forth until it relaxed. Then he rubbed a hand over his face in frustration. Was this a true vision or just a dream?

Whatever he had just witnessed, either true or made up, he knew he was losing time. He needed to return to Genoa quickly. Today.

The room was cast in shadows, and he saw the heavy curtains had been drawn over the windows, cutting out the view of the falls. Moving to stand, he was shocked when a soft moan came from next to him.

He turned quickly and smiled when he saw Rey, still fully clothed, lying on the bed next to him. Ben's book was draped across her lap, as if she had fallen asleep deep within its story. Her dark hair was spread across the pillow and her face relaxed. Her dark eyelashes were closed, and her breathing was even.

He wondered how he had ever fallen asleep with her next to him and smiled as she gave a little snoring sound.

"Cats, I love you," he said softly, and he felt his frustration build again. "Sooner or later, we will deal with this," he warned her sleeping form and then quietly turned and walked into the bathroom to clean for the day.

Zander's mood improved when he found the massive

shower. Twenty minutes under the hot water helped ease some of his tense muscles.

He also had new clothes, thanks to Ben. The pants were a little loose around the seat area, but there was a nice black belt that ensured they would stay put. The shirt and jacket were good, and he studied the tie with narrow eyes only once before discarding it.

After he dressed, Rey escaped into the bathroom and took an even longer shower than he had. When she emerged, Zander was pleased to see she wore nice slacks and a poppy-colored top that showcased her arms.

In fact, when they went to the dining room again, he discovered that all his friends now sported new clothing, even Sash. The large warrior had a black shirt that stretched over his huge muscles and tan pants with neat black shoes that had white laces.

They had breakfast in Ben's private dining hall. Eggs, meats, and soft breads were served on silver platters while the warriors from Genoa stretched and yawned about him.

Zander enjoyed the bacon, something he and his family had refrained from since he and Caylee were around six years of age. His twin, who could feel the emotions of many creatures and people alike, had urged the castle to refrain from the killing of animals. This was welcomed by their mother, and Zander found some of his favorite meals were lacking in meat, except fish, which Caylee claimed had no thoughts or feelings that she could detect.

"Slept like a baby," Seth said from across the table from Zander. "Never knew a bed could be so soft."

"Snored like crazy," Kenzo grumbled as he stuffed more eggs in his mouth. "Heard him through the walls."

"Good, good. When you are all done, I thought I could give you a tour of the facilities," Ben exclaimed with a smile.

"Ben, we have to go," Zander said with a shake of his head. Disappointment crossed the man's face before he smiled again.

"Of course, but first…"

"No. We have to go right after this meal," Zander said firmly. He saw anger cross Ben's face first, then the man looked down and Zander realized he was sad.

"Ben, we can only imagine how long you have waited for us, but Zander is right, we must get back to Genoa," Rey stated as she placed a hand on top of Ben's, which was sitting on the table.

"I know, deep down I know. But it still hurts that I only get one night with you, my friends." Ben squeezed Rey's hand. "Yes, we will go as soon as possible."

"As soon as possible" was a lot longer than Zander wanted.

Ben told them that the tear was located in a secret cavern behind the waterfall, and it should only be accessed at night. This restriction allowed him to ensure the secrecy of the cavern from the hotel's guests and workers.

"We have had issues in the past," Ben informed them as they finished breakfast. Ben spoke of guests finding the cavern and trying to access the barrier that led into Genoa. He also spoke of creatures, evil creatures from Genoa, having crossed the barrier in the past. "I have had to put several wards around the tear." He told them a story of a nasty Bough dog escaping into the surrounding forest.

Zander's dream or vision of his twin kept replaying in

his head. The image had caused an uncontrollable urge to hurry. He found his frustration building all through the meal after he learned of the needed delay in returning home.

Caylee's words came back to him as they were leaving the table, and he quickly asked Belent and Ben if they had ever heard of Pescara.

"Pescara?" Belent repeated with a shake of his head. "Is it in Genoa?"

"I think it's an island," Zander replied as Rey came up next to them.

"Pescara?" she asked, tilting her head. "Why would you want to go there? It's full of brigands."

"You know where Pescara is?" Zander asked as he spun to look at her.

"Sure, all good dragon riders know the far island," she said with a small lift of her shoulders.

"How about Trillium?" Zander asked, trying to remember the details of his vision. Now that Rey had confirmed there was such a place as Pescara, he knew that what he'd had was a vision and not a dream.

"No," Rey said thoughtfully, shaking her head. "I don't know that place."

"The tower," Zander said. He paused, "I can't remember the name. But she mentioned a tower."

"Yes, the Della Val," Rey said with a nod. "I have heard of it, but not many riders go out beyond our own islands. We don't like to be confined to ships and you cannot get out that far riding on a dragon."

"Far?" Zander asked as fear ate away at him. "How far?"

"Kenzo would know better. I hear he grew up on the long island." Rey waved the large man over. Kenzo had shaved his head again, and his red dragon tattoo glowed against his dark skin as they stood in the dining room's bright lights. "Kenzo, how many days does it take to get to Pescara from the cliffs?" she asked.

"Pescara? A good captain would drive his crew hard to reach the Straight of Nereis by the third day. As long as they don't stop at Eras, their journey should be safe." Kenzo rubbed at a large hoop on his left ear. "There are fewer laws on Eras. It's a small island, but it is close to the long island, and from there it's only another two days travel."

"Have you heard of Trillium?" Zander asked and felt concerned when Kenzo shook his head no. "How about a captain named Rouen?"

"Bryce Rouen?" Here Kenzo laughed heartily and smiled. "Yes, I know of him."

"So, he's real?" Zander asked quickly.

"Oh yeah, he's real, a real scoundrel," Kenzo said with another laugh and a shake of his head. "There are more trustworthy captains. You might be better to go with Captains Jade or Franks. I'm not saying he's a bad captain, he would get you to your destination, but you would find the price doubled if you wanted to get home safely," Kenzo said with another laugh that had Zander's mouth going dry with concern for his sister.

"So, he's a brigand?" Zander demanded and gritted his teeth.

"No, he's not a pirate," Kenzo said with a shake of his head. "He hates them. Captain Rouen won't have any man on his ship whose ever been known to deal with a brigand."

"I believe he's taking my sister to Pescara," Zander said, studying the man. "Do you know if she will be safe with him?"

When Kenzo cleared his throat and looked uncomfortable, Zander's eyes narrowed at the man, much as his eyes had narrowed during his vision.

"Well," Kenzo said after taking a deep breath, "let's just say she will have the time of her life. But yes, if the price is right, Captain Rouen will return her safely to home."

Zander didn't take much comfort in Kenzo's assurance, but until he was safely back at home himself, he could do nothing about his sisters, nor his parents.

His worry continued all through the tour Ben gave him and Rey of the hotel. The others wanted to explore the village, so the large group had split into three smaller ones. Belent joined Zander's group, invisibly of course.

"There are many shops in the village, but we also have two here in the building. This comes in helpful when winter storms close down the road to town," Ben told them as they walked out of the lobby and turned left down a large hallway. "There are three restaurants too, all overseen by Chef Parker. I was lucky to steal him away from California."

"You seem to enjoy running things here," Rey said with a smile.

"Ah, well, after the hardships of my former years, I have come to the conclusion that you shouldn't do anything you don't enjoy," Ben said with a smile.

"Do you find you enjoy Earth?" Zander asked, thinking briefly of his mother's stories of her time trapped here.

"It has its advantages." Ben stopped as he thought for a minute before finally continuing. "Yes, there are many differences between the two worlds, but here the technology has advanced, giving far more comforts. I do miss the *magic*." Ben whispered the last word and gave them a quick wink. "And I find that living at a different age rate is confusing."

"Speaking of," Rey said. She wrapped her hands around Ben's arm as they walked. "Your Ms. Stratton is quite a fine lady."

"Ah," Ben said with a smile. "Yes, Shelly has, despite my first impressions, become the heart of Twisted Pines."

"Ben, why did you call the hotel that?" Belent asked. His voice came from beside Zander's left elbow, causing him to jolt slightly then laugh at himself for completely forgetting the sorcerer had joined them on the tour.

"Don't you see it?" Ben asked. He turned suddenly on the spot to peer beyond Zander to where the invisible man stood. "It's Castle Pines, just smaller and twisted a bit. The main floor plans are the same, with some adjustments for technology like the elevators."

"I thought so when we drove here. It reminded me of home," Zander explained with a smile. "But why?"

The smile on Ben's face fell away for a minute, and they all could see the time that had passed on his face. When he spoke, it was in a small whisper.

"The first few years of being here were hard on me. I missed Genoa, I missed home, I missed you all." Ben cleared his throat once before continuing. "It took ten years before the hotel could be started. During that time, I lived in a small cottage, which is still here. I lived alone, and my days and nights were lonely."

Zander saw Rey give the man's arm a squeeze. Ben looked down at her hand and gave her a smile before continuing.

"Is that when you wrote your books?" Rey asked, and Ben smiled.

"Ah, you've been reading my latest," he stated with a nod. "Yes, the sales from the books allowed me to build. When the hotel was finished, I was well over being a hermit," he said with another nod of his head. "I needed to be in the middle of things, of life. I fear I was quite a wild man back then. Of course, it was the sixties." Another wink, this one sent to Rey, and then he laughed at their lack of understanding. "It was a wild and crazy time. But, by a few years later I had much to deal with beyond partying."

"Trouble?" Rey asked.

"Oh, not so much, but the tear seemed to be a beacon for trouble." Ben started walking again. "I had several, shall we call them, adventures?"

"And Ms. Stratton?" Rey prodded.

"Oh, Shelly came on about forty years ago," Ben said with a sigh. "Young and full of ideas. She came to the inn as an intern and, before a year was up, I had hired her as my manager." Zander saw a smile form on his friend's face as he thought back. "She had her fingers in every nook and cranny of this inn. Of course, I tried to keep my magic and the tear secret from her, but that didn't last long."

"What happened?" Rey asked.

"She discovered my secret," Ben said with a shake of his head. "Almost killed me when she did too."

17

THE FALLS

Zander was amazed by the massive hotel Ben had established near the rip between Earth and Genoa. The similarities between his home, Castle Pines, and this building were there, but there were also small differences.

Here, there were pools and a spa where one could be pampered. Stores and dining halls stood where exercise yards were at home. But there was a duplicate ballroom where they had one at home. The one at home sported goldleaf trimming and a large crystal chandelier where Ben's had marble trimming and glass.

In Castle Pines, there were training courtyards and stables. And the village was different too—stone homes with gardens behind their gates. Here there was less livestock. Genoa's many creatures were missing, and horses had been replaced by cars. Zander found himself missing home very much by the time their tour was finished.

"Should we be concerned about General Wilberg here?" Rey asked as they returned to the hotel.

"The general will have difficulty crossing the border," Ben stated with a shake of his head. "The US government might try and use their alliance with Canada to continue the search, but since you will be leaving tonight, they will have nowhere to look."

"But what about you?" Zander asked.

"Me?" Ben asked with a laugh. "I am a resident of Canada, have been for the past sixty years, according to my birth certificate."

"What if they trace us here?" Rey asked.

"I have already had your van taken north. I had a trusted employee, Mr. Isleton, who is head of my security, take the van himself. Nothing beyond that will trace you to me. And if it does, my family has owned this land for two generations."

"You don't fear discovery?" Zander asked.

"It won't be the first time I have come close, and it won't be the last," Ben said with a shake of his head.

They had lunch at one of the pretty tables along the patio. Zander had a fish Ben called "trout," which melted in his mouth. There was also some long grain rice and vegetables that were a bright green, which he thought an odd color.

They talked of times in Genoa, times which Ben seemed to miss. Rey asked him about his books, and he confirmed that most of them were based on his adventures in Genoa.

"I twisted the story, much like my inn. Things are similar, but different," he explained with a smile.

After lunch, the whole group met to gather their supplies and go over their plan.

"I don't know where the tear is located in Genoa. I have the impression it's in the vast wilderness far to the north of the Pontella," Ben informed them as he helped them pack dried meats and cheeses into new backpacks. "You might need to carry water too. Half of those who have found their way here are immensely thirsty."

"How many have crossed over?" Seth asked as he stuffed an extra shirt into his backpack.

"Less than a lot and more than some," Ben said with a smile. "Don't fret for me, my friend. I am kept busy here."

"What else can you tell us?" Rey asked.

"I have had years to think," Ben said as he turned to study Zander. "The mist, I think it was all for you and your family. But I think the trap at the stones was for you alone."

"We think there were tests done prior to our reaching the stones," Belent stated with a nod of his head.

"Yes, tests were done, but none of those people have come here. I think they, along with your parents, were sent to another land. Maybe one across the borders Genoa set on that world." Ben held up a hand as everyone started to throw questions at him. "I only have my guesses, nothing solid, but I think the queen and king were sent somewhere other than here. I came to this conclusion only after I had a brief encounter with Anna here on Earth."

"Mom?" Zander asked quickly. He stood from the chair he had just sat down in. "You saw my mother?"

"Yes. It was over thirty years ago, but yes, I sought her out," Ben said with a smile. "She was living in the Washington area near Seattle."

"*Mom?*" Zander whispered and shook his head as he listened to Ben's story.

"I didn't let her see me at first. I was fearful that I would change her history and I couldn't do that, no matter what," Ben said with conviction. "But I saw her interact with several, shall we call them, questionable people. She was living on the streets and using a small amount of magic to gain income. No, I won't tell you too much, but her use of the magic is what brought me to her."

"Did you talk to her?" Zander asked.

"Yes, briefly," Ben said with a sigh. "She stole my wallet." The laugh that came out of Ben was so loud and unexpected that Zander soon found himself laughing too. "I never saw her do it, and to this day I'm still amazed by that."

"What else happened?" Zander quickly asked as he tried to imagine his mother taking anything that didn't belong to her.

"Nothing. I tried to find her the next day, just to check up on her, but she had already moved. It was a good thing too because when I went back to that corner, the whole homeless camp had been cleared away by the police. I'm sure the general had something to do with it, and I was glad your mother was no longer there."

"He hunted her for years," Zander stated with a shake of his head.

"Yes, but now she is beyond his reach. I felt when Wizard Leian came into Earth, and I also felt when he and Anna left a few days before you came."

"How can that be?" Belent asked as the two sorcerers stared at each other.

"I have thought about that too. The only thing I can think of is that the red mists used to transport us here caused a time rift," Ben explained with a shake of his head.

"So, the red mist might have sent the queen and king somewhere else and some*time* else?" Belent asked.

"I guess you will need to find that out," Ben said, his eyes fixed on Belent.

Their evening meal was served in the private dining room again. There was more fish and a deep browned meat that they all enjoyed with a rich side sauce.

When Ms. Stratton joined them, Zander noticed with alarm that her face was white and her brown eyes wide with fear. She quickly shut the door behind her and rushed to Ben's side.

"The sheriff called to tell me that he received a call from a lieutenant general about a missing Indian reservation van," Shelly said as she glanced down the table. Everyone grew quiet at her words.

"Ah, how is Mike?" Ben asked calmly.

"His arthritis is acting up again, but Ben, he had to tell them the van drove up here," she said, her face lined with worry.

"Yes, well, we might need to move along well before dark," Ben said as he wiped his mouth with a napkin. "Go ahead and get things ready for me, dear."

Shelly nodded once and moved to leave. Before she left the room, however, she turned and gave everyone a strained smile. "It was really nice to meet you all. I hope your travels home are safe." With that, she left quickly, shutting the door behind her.

"Ben?" Rey asked as she moved to stand from her chair.

"No, no. Please finish the meal first," Ben advised, reaching over to pat Rey's hand. "Shelly with have your things gathered and waiting for us at the entrance."

"Entrance?" Zander asked.

Ben's smile broadened. "My boy, my home has many secrets only a few know about," Ben said with a laugh.

The secrets were hidden passageways. Zander smiled

when he thought of the dark tunnels inside his own home in Genoa. 'Narnia' his mother had called them. Most led to storerooms that held supplies and were used by servants, but there were a few truly hidden passageways that only the royal family knew of.

There were two of these secret passageways in the family quarters that led down out of the castle, while a third led to the stables where the horses were kept. Their mother had insisted on these, and Zander had always wondered about her urgency to keep these hidden. However, now that he had spent time on the run from forces that hoped to capture him and his friends, he no longer wondered. After all, his mother had spent more time here on Earth running from General Wilberg and his men.

As the light outside the windows quickly faded, Zander fingered the tomahawk he kept tucked into his belt. The stone of the blade felt cold to the touch as he rubbed his fingers over the thin leather straps that kept the stone attached to the wood.

As a pretty pink color bloomed outside, highlighting the impressive mountains, the lights inside the room brightened automatically. Time seemed to slow, and Zander found he no longer was interested in finishing the meal, but instead was once again anxious to be on his way home.

"I have kept you long enough," Ben finally said with a rather dramatic sigh that made Zander think he yearned to keep them, despite the need for a quick departure. "Come, your things will be ready."

Ben led the group out of the dining room and down a narrow hallway that Zander hadn't yet traveled before. The hallway ended at a large table where their things were piled. Foods had been packed, and Zander smiled when he saw several boxes of granola bars.

"Please give these to the queen when you find her. I believe these were her favorites when she lived here," Ben said with a smile. "I have hope that you will find her and your father soon."

Coats were provided and they were told that they would hold off moisture well, despite the material being thin. They had a soft lining inside and felt like the blankets that were rolled and tied to each backpack.

"There are extra clothes inside as well. I just wish I knew where the tear was in Genoa," Ben said with a shake of his head.

Before they were finished loading up, Ms. Stratton was back. Zander saw her hands shake as she reached Ben.

"They are on the road," he heard her hiss in Ben's ear.

Ben gave a short nod. "You know what to do," he said, and they all watched as she quickly left the hallway again.

Quickly, Ben opened the left-hand drawer half an inch and then slammed it back into place. Zander was confused by his actions and squinted his eyes as the man repeated the steps two more times. As the table and wall drew backwards, Zander's face broke out in a grin.

"For when I need a quick escape," Ben exclaimed with a chuckle, but Zander noticed his smile didn't reach his eyes.

The passageway wasn't dark or even made of stone. Instead, there were bright wood-paneled walls and a carpeted floor that was lit by pretty glass domes along the ceiling. The hallway was ten feet in length and there were stairs leading downwards at its end.

At first the stairs were straight, but after fifty steps, they met a sharp turn to their right. Here the wood ended, and stone walls started. Again, they climbed downwards for fifty steps before reaching another angle. This one was at an odd slant, and Zander could feel the air grow cold around them.

They passed two wooden doors nestled along the stairs before they reached the end of the steps, where a large metal door stood. Ben pulled out a key ring with several iron keys and, after searching for a minute, finally found the right key.

"When we cross the lawn, we should be out of sight of the hotel windows, but we will still need to refrain from using any lights until we reach the cave." He handed Belent a long tube. "It's a flashlight. You each have one in your pack. I think we can use them when we reach the cavern."

Zander's fingers itched to reach in his bag for his own flashlight just to study it, but Ben had already unlocked the door and the others were pushing him forward.

Ms. Stratton's words echoed in his mind. *"They are on the road."* Images of General Wilberg flashed in his mind and worry filled him.

Rey grabbed his hand and pulled him towards the fresh air. He quickly blinked several times to get his eyes to adjust to the sudden darkness. It appeared the sun had set fully while they were hidden in the windowless stairwell.

A large bush hid Ben's secret door and its branches scratched them as they moved along the building's outer walls. Shadows and lights mixed beyond the safety of the bush as the hotel windows shone yellow. Every once in a while, Zander could hear far-off laughter from the outdoor patio on the other side of the building.

Ben confirmed no one was near and quickly urged the group forward. They quietly raced across the lawn towards the forest, which sat between the falls and the hotel. One glance backwards towards the road confirmed all their fears. A long line of red flashing lights was creeping along the lower mountain's valley, heading closer to them.

The quiet drumming of the fall's waters could be heard

off to their right. It grew louder the further they raced. It seemed miles to Zander, but it was only yards before their company came to a halt.

"Here," Ben said breathlessly as he brought them to a rather large tree trunk. "After the rocks, we turn right. But first, where is the tomahawk?"

"Here, I have it." Zander lifted it from his belt.

"Good, hold on tight. You won't need to use; you just need to have it at this time to pass through the rip. And, I believe you will have need of it before too long." Ben turned to Belent. "The tear will strip you of your magic, it always does me." He clasped a hand on Belent's shoulder. "This only lasts a while, but because I don't know what dangers you will face on the other side, you all might want to enter the tear with your weapons drawn."

With a quiet nod, he moved out of the tree's protection and led them through the shrubs until they reached a little shed nestled up against the rock walls of the mountains. The sound of the falls was deafening by now, but they still could not see it.

Another key was produced, and Zander read signs on the door talking of danger and electrical shock. When the door opened, Ben led them all inside and quickly shut the door again.

Zander was shocked to see that it wasn't a shed they stood in, but a large cavern.

"My magic keeps this shed's illusion in place. I have had too many tourists wander into the caves," Ben said as he clicked on his flashlight and showed Belent how to work his own.

The cavern was round and grew smaller the further in it went. Belent stumbled once, but Ben was there to help him. It felt like the very ground itself shook with anger, and

Zander realized it was their closeness to the falls that made the cavern shake.

"It always hits me here too," Ben said, patting Belent's arm.

"I'm cold," Belent stated in reply as Rey moved forward to help the sorcerer.

"Yes, but we are almost there," Ben urged, pointing off into the darkness. "See?"

It took a second before Zander saw what the man was pointing at, but when he did, his eyes opened with amazement.

Settled inside the cavern at its far end was a vertical slit. The glowing blue tear was ten feet in front of the backside of the waters of Fairy Falls.

18

HOME

Rey's mind was filled with the need to rush forward into the cavern and enter the glowing tear. The tear was a dark blue rip that seemed to hover two feet above the ground. The edges rippled slightly before they melted into the wall of the cave.

Despite the need to rush, as always, her first priority was her ward, the prince of Genoa, Zander. Standing next to Belent, she felt the sorcerer go limp and called Sash over so the large warrior could help her.

"Here, take him while I go in first." She turned quickly when Zander rushed forward.

"No," he said as he grabbed her arm.

"If there is danger, I go first. I am your protector," she growled as he shook his blond head.

"You are only my protector when we are on dragons, not here, not this time," he replied. They both spun when a loud growl came from Seth.

"Oh, for pity's sake, I will go first." And with this, he walked across cold dirt floor of the cavern and right up to the tear. He turned once and gave them a smile and a wink. "See you in Genoa."

And then he stepped backwards into the tear and disappeared.

"Me next," Corbin said as he quickly grabbed Avaline's hand and raced towards home.

"Quickly, the army will be here soon," Ben urged. He turned to where Belent still stood, aided by the large warrior Sash. "Take care of them and do not give any thought to me. I am happy."

"But what will you tell them?" Rey asked as she stood next to Zander, her hand still on his arm.

"I will tell them the truth; you are no longer here. Now go."

The warriors formed a line with Rey and Zander in the middle of the group, each with their weapons drawn and tense. As they disappeared, one by one, Rey felt her nerves rise and her muscles tense. She kept her free hand in Zander's and quickly pushed through the tear first.

Her ears popped and she felt an intense inward pressure on her entire body. Her vision went black and, as she continued to move forward, all her senses lessened until she thought she would pass out. Before she could suck in another breath, however, everything returned to normal, and the world around her sharpened and grew brighter.

"Here, let me help you," Seth said, and she felt a hand on her arm, lifting her. "Knocked me on my ass for a second too," he said with a chuckle.

"Zander?" she mumbled quickly.

"Here, I'm here," Zander said, and she turned and saw his face float next to her as the world grew even brighter.

"Here, here's some water," Kenzo said, and she drank from the bottle he handed her.

"Are we all here?" she asked as she handed the water to Zander.

"All accounted for," Belent said, but his voice sounded weak.

"Where are we?" She blinked several times before the forest around them came into focus.

"Looks like the Helmand mountains," Seth said as he peered around. "But sharper."

She saw Zander hand the water to Kylo and turned to look at the surrounding mountains herself. Snow topped the sharp purple peaks and green trees lined their feet. When she saw the familiar moons in the sky of her home world, she took a deep breath of relief.

So, they were home, Genoa. She spun on the spot and saw a familiar peak.

"We are along the Karakuls," she said with a smile. The Karakuls were the mountains on Genoa's northern border. It protected the mainland from the other dangerous lands Genoa had separated hundreds of years before, a separation that kept Genoa's creatures safe from those who had traveled to the planet from another. Those who would cause harm to Genoa's children. "Somewhere between Valorna and the Pontella is my guess."

"Yes, I see it now," Seth stated as he helped Mateo up from the ground.

"Okay, we know where we are, but how do we get home now?" Zander asked with his hands on his hip.

They ended up walking south towards the river the rest of that day. They saw no one this far north and spent that night in a rock clearing at the base of Pe Leon, one of the tallest mountains in the range.

"Once in Valorna, we can see who's stationed there and get rides back to Castle Pines," Zander advised as he handed Rey a bowl of stew he had been served. "I can be home in two days' time."

"I wonder how much time has passed," she mused after she took her first bite of the dark stew.

"Time?" Zander asked and turned to look at Belent.

"I fear Rey is right." The sorcerer, who was looking more like himself now, turned his brown eyes on Zander. "We have been gone around a week of Genoa's time, however with the red mist throwing us back near your mother's departure on Earth, I fear we may have gone back or even forward in time."

"But is that possible?" Seth asked as he dished another bowl for Zander.

"The stars appear close to our own time, but I have not spent enough time studying them to know for sure," Belent said with a shake of his head.

They talked for several more hours about their pending travels the next day and how they would return to Castle Pines. Yet with each minute, Rey saw Zander's frustration grow. When he moved off to take up his watch, she followed him.

"What bothers you?" she asked as they settled on the rock several yards off from the fire and the others. Their backs were to the light, and they faced the darkness and the forest.

"What was this all for?" he finally answered.

She tilted her head. "For?" she finally asked after several moments of silence.

"This." He waved a hand back at the camp. "We went to the stones to track down the mist. To find who or what it was, and we have accomplished nothing." His last word exploded, and she could feel him vibrate with anger. "Here we are, back in Genoa, and I have no answers."

"But we did return," she said calmly, placing a hand on his arm.

"But my parents, my sisters. Where are they? Charlotte said she was traveling to hell, she said Caylee was also in danger. But what of them? And where are my parents?"

"We will find them." She gave his arm a squeeze.

"But what of the mist?" he asked.

"We will find out what it is, but for now, you must return home. Safe," she urged.

"I worry." He slowly lowered his head until it rested on her shoulder. "I worry for them."

Three days after walking through the tear, they reached Castle Pines. They arrived by dragon, thanks to the current battalion stationed in the queen's castle in Valorna, her home city.

Zander's welcome had been intense, and he was quickly told by the captain stationed there that he was the only remaining member of the royal family who wasn't lost or missing.

"Sir, Prince Aiden from Matera resides in Castle Pines at the moment. He was left as proxy by Princess Caylee," the captain had said.

"Cousin Aiden?" Zander said with a smile. *"Any news regarding my family?"*

"None, my lord. Princess Caylee set out many nights ago. We were only told she seeks a talisman," the captain advised.

"The Trillium," Zander said, *now understanding it*

wasn't a place, but an item. He could not gain any more information from the guards posted at Valorna.

Since being told that his cousin was sitting on the throne, his mood had improved considerably. Aiden was King Calob's oldest child. He usually remained in Matera with his family. Zander and Calob were close, but rarely got to spend much time together.

"With Aiden on the throne, I can continue my search for my family," Zander stated to Belent and Rey as they dismounted the borrowed dragons and walked towards the entrance of the castle nearest the dragon yards. "Prepare a new regiment. We will start the hunt as soon as I am able." He turned when Rey didn't spring into action.

"No," she said, planting her feet in the soft dirt, her hands on her hips and a frown on her lips.

"No?" he demanded. He turned to Belent for confirmation.

"I agree with her," Belent advised. He shook his own head.

Before he could argue more, however, a whole battalion of royal guards rushed into the courtyard and surrounded them. They were alarmed by their sudden appearance, but then Zander saw Wizard Leian and his wife Shiarra walking towards them followed by Counselor Ray Fielder.

"Leian, Shiarra?" Zander asked quickly as he shook the wizard's hand. "Ray? What is happening?"

"Sir. We must talk immediately," Counselor Ray answered. With a nod, he ushered them into the castle.

The large procession walked down the hallways of his home. Seeing the castle's defenses set caused a deep worry to settle inside him. Guards stood at every doorway, and the windows, usually opened wide to the breeze, were all closed and barred.

He felt Ray and Belent's presence behind him and took some comfort, but his worry increased when Ray led them to the royal throne room instead of the private chambers usually used for counsel.

"Sir." Counselor Ray turned to face the three. "First, let me say I am glad to see you."

"Ray, what is happening?" Zander demanded.

"Wizard Col discovered the possibility of a window that would show your family's location. He took Princess Caylee to seek this, but that was several weeks ago, and nothing has been heard from them for twelve nights. She has not responded to our Trans Rock summons as of late," Ray said, speaking of the magical rocks formed by wizards that allowed communication from great distance and, if needed, transported one to the other when the rocks were broken. They all turned as Zander's cousin Aiden hurried into the room.

"Zander," Aiden said with a broad smile on his face. Aiden was two years younger than him but just as tall. His dark hair and green eyes spoke of family connections, but the slight tilt of his brows spoke of his mother's fairy heritage.

"Cousin." Zander beamed and embraced Aiden in a warm hug.

"Quickly," Counselor Ray encouraged, causing Zander to turn and look at the older man. "Before the council gets here."

"Zander, you must understand, when your sister disappeared three weeks ago, I was left to battle the council. They have fought my every decision," Aiden said quickly.

"Three weeks," Zander said and turned to study Ray.

"Yes, your highness. Three weeks. It has in fact been five weeks since you yourself left to inspect the stones."

"Hurry," Aiden hissed. "They were right behind me."

"The council is wanting to crown you. Tonight." Wizard Leian grabbed Zander's arms.

"Crown?" Zander asked with a shake of his head. "No. My parents..."

"Have not been seen for over five weeks. Most consider them dead," Shiarra insisted.

"But—" Zander started.

"Your sisters are missing too. The council has been in turmoil since then. Even the council from Prince Aiden has been in question," Counselor Ray continued. "Most have started to listen to Counselor Blake, who raises questions about every order the prince has made of late."

"He's doubted my every move, you mean," Aiden said with a frown.

"But to crown me?" Zander asked with panic. He knew he wasn't ready, not while his family was missing, not dead. He knew he wouldn't be ready, not for years.

"The council calls for leadership. Either from you or from Counselor Blake," Aiden said firmly.

"He means to dethrone the royals?" Rey demanded as she moved to stand next to Zander.

"No. But he aims to rule in their absence," Wizard Leian stated with a shake of his head just as the chamber's doors opened wide.

"Ah," Counselor Blake stated. He was a tall, yellow-haired man with a bushy mustache of fine orange and yellow. His bright orange eyes blinked sideways, as sand sprites usually did. "So, the rumors are true, Your Highness."

Twelve others entered behind Counselor Blake, including two sprites, a rather large tree sprite and a smaller water sprite. Zander could also see two wind willows, a gnome, and a troll amongst the several humans.

"Counselors," Zander said with a nod of his head. "I have just now returned."

"Welcome back," Blake said with a toothy smile. "There is much to discuss."

"Agreed. But first—" Zander started.

"Urgency is required," Blake urged, and his odd eyes blinked again.

"My cousin has just returned from a long journey; surely court matters can wait," Aiden interjected.

"Normally, yes, I would be the first to agree. However —" Blake shook his head mournfully.

"There is a matter of leadership," the water sprite said from behind Blake.

"Leadership?" Zander said with a shake of his head. "It is my understanding that Princess Caylee left my cousin, Prince Aiden, in charge while she was away."

"Ah, that is the topic we must discuss," Blake said, and Zander saw the toothy grin again.

"Your Highness, we require something more permanent," the water sprite stated. Zander searched for the creature's name and could only come up with the word 'Dollop.'

"Derlop is correct," Blake stated with a grave nod. "We, I mean the people of Genoa, require assurance that the land will continue to be ruled by one in authority." Blake's odd eyes traveled to Aiden and the toothy smile faltered. "Competently."

Zander had no doubt that the last word was intended as an insult to his cousin and quickly stepped forward.

"Agreed," Zander stated and held his hands up. "However, I will not be crowned king until it has been confirmed my parents are dead."

"But we require—" Blake started and quickly stopped when Zander held his hands higher.

"I, however, will assure the council that I will remain here in Castle Pines. Despite my urgency to return to the quest of finding my missing family," Zander said.

"Ah," Blake said as he rubbed long thin fingers over his mustache. "But that is a problem. Most are seeking a king, not a crown prince, to rule."

"What would you have me do?" Zander asked after a deep breath.

The demands were long and tedious. After Zander's question, Blake had pulled a long parchment from his outer pocket and immediately started listing the council's requirements as Zander moved to sit on his small throne adjacent to his families' empty ones.

However, before the tenth demand was listed, a headache formed behind Zander's left eye. As Blake started on the eleventh demand, Zander once again raised his hands.

"How about a compromise."

The council members went quiet.

"A compromise?" Blake asked, and Zander heard suspicion in his voice.

"Yes." Zander stood and walked over to look in the odd eyes for a second before turning away. "I will not sit on my parents' thrones, but what if I give the people a royal wedding?"

"A wedding?" Blake asked.

"And just who will you be marrying?" Rey demanded from her sitting place along the outer wall.

"A wedding." Zander held his hand up to stop the loud murmur amongst those gathered in the room. "That will take place before the night is over."

"A wedding. Your marriage might appease the people of Genoa. It would show good faith that you intend to remain, here and in charge," Blake said thoughtfully as he gave his mustache another rub. "Yes, that will do nicely."

"And these other requirements?" Zander asked, his head tilted towards the group.

"Will be set aside. For now," Blake said with a nod.

"Then it is settled," Counselor Ray said loudly, clapping Blake on his skinny back. "Now, let's leave these two alone." He almost pushed the sand sprite out the door. They were closely followed by the other counselors.

"Whom do you intend to marry?" Rey asked again as Zander turned to study her. Her dark eyes were narrow, and he thought he saw a hint of anger behind them. Or was it fear?

She once again wore her dragon warrior leathers, pants the color of deep brown with an orange strip down their sides and a soft tunic of the same orange. Her long black hair was braided in a single strand down her back. His fingers itched to reach out and feel how soft it was, but he refrained.

"Rey," he started, but he stopped when she quickly shook her head and put her hands up in defense.

"No." Her single word caused a deep panic to set in his stomach. "You don't mean this. Do you?"

With relief he smiled and understood finally that it was fear in her eyes, not rejection. "You know I do," he whispered as he drew closer.

"You do?" she asked when he stopped inches from her.

"I do." He smiled at the words and the meaning behind them as he drew in for a long overdue kiss.

That night, as the heat of the day waned and the sun cast long shadows along the ground, Zander Brigdon Haddock, crown prince of Genoa, stood waiting for his bride. He was surrounded by his friends and the high council of Castle Pines, along with most of the village people and creatures of Genoa who called Pinewoods their home.

He stood in his royal dark green uniform with its brass buttons and his medals and dragon sash across his chest. His best friend, Corbin, and his cousin, Aiden Edward Haddock, lined the front of the small dais that sat in the front courtyard of the castle. The courtyard allowed a large gathering of over a thousand, and it appeared no one was missing the royal wedding, despite the short notice.

Sorcerer Belent stood behind him, waiting to officiate the marriage. As the music started, all those gathered turned to watch the bride arrive.

Reyleen Brelanna was dressed in a shining orange dress. Her dragon insignias shone along her breast. Her long dark hair had been braided in piles, which sat atop her head in coils. The flowers she carried had been handpicked by Zander after their private meeting in the throne room. Dragon's lace and heart strands were entwined with ribbons and gems.

Wizard Shiarra walked behind the bride, and she stood in place of Zander's missing family while Reyleen's own family stood behind her. Her mother, Stria, the warrior who had traveled down into the Kylix with his own mother years ago, was still beautiful and said to still be quick with her knife. Her father, Farin, the large cave expert who had also traveled into the Kylix, smiled next to his wife while their other three children, all dragon warriors, stood behind them.

During the wedding, Zander's only regret was that his family wasn't there to witness the most amazing moment of his life. But he vowed that they would be found, either by him or by the four brigades of troops he'd sent out only two hours before his wedding.

One brigade was led by Wizard Leian. They traveled to Tharian to seek counsel from the wizard's council there regarding the mist and its origins.

Another, led by Sash, was traveling to the small camp of Parian, where the mist had first been sighted. Sash was to inspect the camp and seek any information about the trap and mists. Also, he hoped to discover more about the family who had disappeared.

The third was to be led by Seth, who was traveling to Rigel City far in the south. He was going to seek the counsel of King Malicky. Malicky was knowledgeable in all things magical in Genoa and, with his elven magic, might know more about the mists.

The last, which would leave in the morning, would be led by Zander's best friend, Corbin. Corbin would lead the longest journey. He would travel to the Kylix and seek guidance from the goddess herself. Each would be sent with Trans Rocks to keep Zander informed of their progress.

After their vows were over, the bride and groom kissed and embraced for the first time as husband and wife. Before the celebration started, Zander, crown prince of Genoa turned and addressed those gathered, holding his bride's hand in his.

"I now make another vow, this one to you, the people of Genoa. I will not rest until my family, the queen and king and my sisters, are found and returned home safely." He turned and, with Rey's hand in his, walked off the dais and into the next chapter of his life.

The dark and damp cell was no longer empty, or just filled with rats. Two new specimens had been thrown into the cell only minutes before. These were creatures the sorceress had waited for a long time.

Baring her teeth, Io Maltesea hissed with pleasure as the large male lurched forward towards her, no doubt trying to protect the smaller one, the queen.

"*Queen*," Io Maltesea sneered then laughed. "Queen of nothing," she teased as her red eyes continued to study her prisoners.

"Sorceress, we lost six to that one, and two died at the female's hands," her minion Balt grumbled. He exposed his razor-sharp teeth at the man behind the bars. Balt's weapons, which were strapped over his massive chest, glinted as he reached for a short sword with his clawed hand.

"Harm either and I'll have your head," Io Maltesea warned. She was pleased when the creature's hand slipped from his knife back to his hairy side. Then she turned from him to glance back at her prize prisoners.

"Welcome, *Your Majesties*," she sneered as she surrounded herself with her red magic for visual affect. "To hell."

She emitted a deep laugh when she saw true fear fill their eyes. Her long laughter echoed along the stone walls, causing the other prisoners in her dungeon to shriek in fear.

ALSO BY JJ ANDERS

ABOUT THE AUTHORS

JJ ANDERS

JJ Anders is the pseudonym used by the powerhouse writing duo of NY Times & USA Today bestselling author, Jill Sanders and her identical twin sister, Jody. Hailing from the Pacific Northwest, these two talented ladies have merged their creative forces to craft an amazing new fantasy series that will leave you begging for more.

With over sixty bestselling romance books and counting, Jill alone is a force to be reckoned with, boasting thousands of glowing reviews with a cumulative 4.7 star rating. Jody's powerful imagination and newfound love of writing has spawned the thrilling new world and enchanting characters of Genoa. As a furious reader and devoted mother, Jody's passion for storytelling reaches full bloom by teaming up with her talented twin to bring her magical stories to life for the enjoyment of readers everywhere.

 facebook.com/jjandersauthor

twitter.com/jjandersauthor

instagram.com/jjanderauthor

amazon.com/JJ-Anders/e/B074JLJVP4?tag=jillmcom-20

bookbub.com/authors/jj-anders